SO-AWY-429

OUTCAST ON THE COURT

David B. Smith

REVIEW AND HERALD® PUBLISHING ASSOCIATION
HAGERSTOWN, MD 21740

The author assumes full responsibility for the accuracy of all facts
and quotations as cited in this book.

This book was
Edited by Gerald Wheeler
Designed by Bill Kirstein
Cover art by James Martin
Type set: 11/12 Optima

PRINTED IN U.S.A.

R&H Cataloging Service
Smith, David B.
  Outcast on the court.

  I. Title. II. Series.
      813

ISBN 0-8280-0639-3

The Bucky Stone Series
1. *Making Waves at Hampton Beach High*
2. *Showdown at Home Plate*
3. *Outcast on the Court*

CHAPTER ONE

ALONE AT GRADUATION

The PA system of Hampton High's athletic stadium repeated for the third time the familiar strains of "Pomp and Circumstance" as yet another cluster of black-robed seniors marched in awkward cadence down the center aisle formed by the long rows of folding chairs. Bucky twisted in his seat to see how many more remained at the back of the brightly-lit athletic field.

"Seems like a million of 'em," Lisa whispered.

"Yeah." He turned back around and glanced at the girl sitting next to him. "Three more years," he muttered, half to himself.

"Uh huh." She scooted a bit closer, sliding her hand into the crook of his elbow. "Seems like a long way off, but I guess it'll be here before we know it."

The last notes faded away in the cool evening air and the huge block of mortarboards and tassels dipped like a Pacific Ocean wave as the seniors sat down in their reserved seats. Just behind them was this year's junior class. Seated near the back was Sam, Bucky's Vietnamese friend.

As Hampton Beach's principal stood up and began to address the large crowd, Bucky shifted his gaze to the far corner of the athletic field. Now in twilight shadows, the baseball diamond sprawled empty and forlorn.

A sudden stab of resentment shot through him as he remembered the Friday evening just two weeks earlier. Leading in the championship game against the rival Hornets, Bucky had been unceremoniously ordered from the ballfield—by his own coach—for refusing to play after sundown.

With Coach Brayshaw's raging dismissal still vivid in his mind, he had slowly ridden home in the twilight. There he had waited anxiously for news of the game's outcome, hoping that somehow the Panthers could hang on and win without the team's two hottest hitters.

The last ten days of classes after the devastating defeat had slowly ebbed away for Bucky. "Except for Lisa and Sam, all of a sudden, I haven't got a single friend at school," he had sighed wearily to his mother the day finals ended.

Well, there was Dan, Bucky remembered. The star center fielder had been the one player to support him in the aftermath of the Sabbath controversy. In fact, Dan had come up to him the following Monday and, after some hesitation, even asked some questions about his beliefs.

Since then, however, Dan had not approached him again. Once or twice Bucky considered whether or not he should try to bring up the topic of Christianity again. "No more of that," he had finally concluded. "You've pushed your religion on people enough for one school year."

Now he sat quietly with his girlfriend, thinking about the future. What would it take to break down the barriers that had suddenly piled up between him and the rest of the student body?

"Stop daydreaming," teased the gentle voice at his shoulder.

He forced a weak smile. "Sorry."

She looked at him, reading his thoughts. "Hey, I'm still here, aren't I?"

He looked at the empty seats on both sides of them, then nodded gratefully. Reaching over, he gently slid her hand down until their two hands clasped tightly. "Boy, I'll tell you—" He paused. "If I didn't have you . . ." He left the thought unfinished.

Up on the platform, Mr. Wallace concluded his welcome. "And now, our senior class sponsor: Mr. Theodore Brayshaw!"

Bucky's head jerked up as the familiar name reverberated through the loudspeakers. Instinctively he began clapping along with the rest of the student body, but his body tensed up as the athletic director strode to the microphone.

"I didn't know he was their sponsor," he whispered to Lisa, his cheeks flushing at the mention of the coach's name. Even two weeks later, he could not erase his mind's constant replay of the angry words, "I want you off this field now, Stone! And I mean for good! This year, next year, forever! Out!"

It seemed odd now, Bucky reflected, to hear Brayshaw's warm words of congratulations to the graduating seniors. The coach had a smooth, friendly style, and the upperclassmen buzzed with appreciation.

"Every year at this time," he grinned, "the title to a certain song comes to my mind. As I look out at this crop of fine-looking graduating Hampton men and women, and as I think of the eight semesters you have put in here—the 36 months, the 720 school days that have transpired since your first baby-faced moments on this campus—that tune by Paul Simon is worthy of our consideration." He paused for dramatic effect. "And the name of that melody? 'Still Crazy After All These Years.'"

Snickers swept through the ranks of robed seniors at the friendly dig. "That's right, Teddy Baby!" hooted a tall, blond senior sitting near the back of the class.

The coach smiled again, then sobered. "It's been a good year," he reflected. "If you ask me, we came within two innings of it being a *great* year."

A low chorus of boos met his last remark. Even the festivities of graduation weekend had not erased the resentment still smoldering on campus. A number of students sitting near Bucky turned in their chairs and gave him a cold look.

His face scarlet, Bucky forced himself to stare straight ahead. "Of all the . . ." His muttered words, audible only to Lisa, faded away.

Coach Brayshaw, realizing too late the reaction he had caused, coughed awkwardly and switched to a more positive note, but the damage had been done. Moments later he concluded his thoughts and sat down. The crowd, still distracted by the reference to the championship game, gave him only a polite smattering of applause.

Bucky sat in his seat, oblivious to the droning of names as seniors walked up onto the platform one by one to receive their diplomas. Coach's barbed words rang in his ears over and over.

"Why don't we get out of here?" he suddenly whispered to Lisa.

"Right now?"

"Uh huh. Why not? After what Brayshaw just said?"

His girlfriend shook her head slightly. "It's almost over," she whispered. "They're already to the T's."

"I hate being here!" His whisper had a catch to it.

"I know. But just hang in there. You'll make things worse if you march out on 'em now." She gave his hand a squeeze. "During the summer this'll all go away."

He shrugged. "I don't know about that."

"Oh, sure. Trust me."

He edged a little closer to her. "I dunno. Somebody's probably in the parking lot right now planting a bomb on my bike."

"Very funny." She gave him a sympathetic little smile. "Still have that wry sense of humor, I see."

Bucky remained silent, but forced an expression that passed for his lopsided grin.

At long last the ceremony ended. As the final name echoed across the grounds, a sustained whoop rose from the seniors as they congratulated each other with handshakes and hugs. Moments later, they bounced jauntily down the center aisle on their way to the receiving line along the back edge of the field.

Long rows of tables contained soft drinks, pretzels, and cookies.

Hand in hand the young couple threaded their way through the crowd. Most ignored them though one or two of the members of the ball team did flash Bucky a sympathetic look.

As he reached the edge of the field, he suddenly found himself face to face with Dan Litton. The two stared at each other with a trace of awkwardness.

Lisa broke the silence first. "Hi, Dan."

"Hi." The powerfully built student studied the young couple before shaking his head ruefully. "Well, ol' Coach took one last shot at us. Right in front of the whole stupid world." His voice remained even, though.

Bucky snorted. "Hey, that jab wasn't for you, and you know it." He tried to mask any bitterness in his voice. "You busted your leg giving your all for the team." He paused. "Everybody on campus knows you had a whale of a year."

"Yeah, so did you," Dan grunted. "Panthers wouldn't even have been leading in that last game if you hadn't been hitting so well."

The younger boy nodded. "Oh, well." He reflected for a moment, then stepped forward and offered his hand. "Listen, have a great summer. And . . . congratulations for a terrific season."

"You too, man."

"I . . ." For a second, he almost said something about their hallway conversation two weeks before, then remembered his earlier resolve. "What are you doin' this summer?"

"Working at the station. Soon as I get this crazy thing off."

"Which one?"

"Unocal. Same as last summer." Dan reached down to scratch around the top edge of his cast. "How about you?"

"Well, I think I have a job lined up at that home improvement center on Landis Road."

Dan grinned. "Over by where you live, right?" he said to Lisa.

"Uh huh." She slapped Bucky gently on the arm. "I suppose you'll be coming over to beg free lunch off me every day."

Bucky laughed. For the first time that evening, he felt himself relaxing.

"Well, I gotta split," Dan told them. "Takes me twice as long to get anywhere, seems like." He took a step away, then turned back. "I'm sure this sounds dumb right now, but are you thinking of playing basketball next fall?"

The question took Bucky completely by surprise. "Huh?"

"JV basketball."

"You've got to be kidding. I'll never play anything in this town again."

Dan shook his head. "Hey, that stuff'll pass. No reason at all why you shouldn't try out for hoops next year."

"Are you planning to?"

"For sure. Basketball's really my game. Power forward."

"You could have fooled me the way you hit a baseball over the fence every third time up."

Dan grinned. "Well, give it some thought."

"No way. Besides," he added as an afterthought, "I'd have the same Friday night problem I just got beat up over." He paused. "I'm not gonna go through that again!"

The older boy thought for a moment. "I don't think this league's games are ever on Friday," he said at last. "Well, maybe playoffs."

"Yeah, that song sounds real familiar," Bucky retorted with a terse growl in his voice. " 'Come on and play, Buck. We can work things out. No problem.' "

Sensing his friend's anger, Dan backed off. "Well, just wait and see."

"No way." Bucky vehemently shook his head. "Not a chance in the world."

* * *

"Ted, I can't believe you said what you did up there!"

The two athletic coaches sat in Mr. Brayshaw's office. Piles of grade sheets and end-of-year reports covered the younger instructor's desk.

"What are you talking about?"

"You know perfectly well what I'm talking about! Bringing up that championship game right during your speech. And with Stone in the crowd! You knew he was there, didn't you?"

"So what?"

Coach Walker leaned over the desk, resting both his hands squarely in the middle of the papers. "It was a tacky thing to do."

Brayshaw shook his head in irritation. "Don't lecture me," he snapped. "When I want you writing my speeches for me, I'll let you know. As for Stone being there, yeah, I knew it. He's a big boy—he can take it."

The older coach straightened. "You're right about

that," he responded, his voice taut. "He can take it. He's proved that these past few weeks."

"Oh, yeah?" Coach Brayshaw began to heat up. "How? By walking out on his own team during the biggest game of the year? What does that prove . . . except that he's a selfish little"—he groped for a word—"screwball?"

"You call a kid a screwball 'cause he has enough guts to follow through on what he believes? Walking off that field at sundown took more courage than either you or I have—or anybody else on the team, for that matter—and we both know it."

"Yeah, what about that sundown business?" Brayshaw demanded. "Is that a crock or what? Shutting down your life just because the sun goes behind a hill."

"It's what he believes," Coach Walker retorted, his voice rising. "Millions of people believe the same thing, so don't get on Stone for that."

"But how many of them carry it so far that they're willing to stick it to their ball team when something like that gets in their way? That's my point." The younger coach was breathing hard, his face red. "I don't care what foolishness a guy like Stone totes around in his head until he brings it onto *my* ballfield and messes up *my* team."

"And *your* championship hopes. That's what this is really all about, isn't it? You just can't let it go, can you?"

Neither one said anything for a moment. Both could feel the tension begin to subside.

"Maybe you're right," Coach Brayshaw admitted at last. "We were so close!" He hit his fist against the desk top and looked away for a moment.

"Hey, I was there, remember?" The older man's voice softened. "I wanted it as badly as you did."

"Yeah." Brayshaw sat glumly, the flush receding from his cheeks. "I admit, I don't understand stuff like this. I mean, where I come from, you go to church on Sunday once in a while—if there isn't a big game on—and if you're good, you go to heaven when you die. That's it, man. Things like this Saturday business, quitting at sundown, and all that . . . I never heard of it before Stone showed up."

Coach Walker said nothing.

The junior varsity coach shook his head. He picked up a box of papers and struggled to his feet. "You're still not going to get me to change my mind about Stone, though."

"That's up to you. I'm just tellin' you this: you lay off him. No more jabs like this morning."

Coach Brayshaw gave a short laugh. "Hey, it's summertime, Herb. I'll leave him alone. The less I see of Mr. Stone the better."

"What're you gonna do if he shows up next year wanting to play again?" Walker looked at his partner. "Or basketball this fall? You seen how tall he is?"

Again Brayshaw laughed. "Not a chance. I scared him off for good, I think."

The older instructor gave him a hard look. "That may be our loss," he said quietly.

CHAPTER TWO

SABBATH AT THE LAKE

"Excuse me, young man, could you help me find some half-inch T-valve sprinkler connectors?" the gray-haired woman asked. "I can't seem to find any in these bins."

Bucky grinned. "Sure. Give me two seconds to get this put away, and I'll be right over."

Climbing up on the second step of the short ladder, he slid the box of hose couplings into their assigned spot on the third shelf. Then he hurried over to where she waited patiently.

"T-valve? I'm sure we have some here somewhere. This is all the half-inch stuff right here. T-valve . . ." His eyes quickly scanned the many rows of bins filled with the various white plastic pipe fittings.

"Here we go!" he exclaimed. "Way at the top."

He reached in and grabbed a handful. "How many do you need?"

The customer searched through a list in her hand. "Just two. My husband is adding some sprinkler lines on the side lawn this afternoon."

"Well, this'll do it for you." Bucky gave her a friendly smile and put the two pieces in her cart.

As she walked away, he reached up with one sleeve to wipe a trace of perspiration from his forehead. Even indoors, it was a muggy summer day. The sweat left a slight stain on his store-assigned orange work jersey.

"Two weeks and I feel like I've been working here all my life," he muttered to himself as he headed toward the small employees' cubicle where there was a drinking fountain. Even after such a brief time on the job he was quickly learning where the store stocked many of its items and could even answer many of the customers' simpler how-to questions.

A glance at the large clock over the drinking fountain indicated half an hour until lunchtime. In between answering questions, Bucky restocked shelves and helped unload two large shipments of 2" x 6" redwood lumber that had just come in.

"Thanks a lot, Stone," grunted the man in charge. The supervisor was a large, overweight man in his thirties. His bulging orange shirt strained at each button.

"Sure." Bucky mopped at his forehead again. Now it was hot! Picking up his sack lunch, he headed out the back door and glanced around for a shady spot.

"Pardon me, I can't seem to find what I'm looking for," a lilting voice interrupted.

He whirled around with a grin. "Hey, what are you doing here? I thought you were baby-sitting again today."

Lisa laughed. "They called at the last minute and backed out. Tomorrow yes, but today no. So I got a day off."

"You'll never get rich that way."

She made a face. "Who needs to be rich when you have good looks like I've got?"

"That's true," he agreed.

"Anyway," she bubbled, "I brought a fantastic lunch for two. And I insist that you join me."

"But I already have a lunch," he protested with a grin. "I made it myself."

"Let me see." Lisa surveyed the scanty contents of his paper bag. "You're really dying to eat that, huh?"

"Well, what have you got?"

She slowly opened up the lid to her picnic basket. Right on top was a huge piece of cherry pie. "Now what do you say? Still salivating to eat that lunch of yours?"

"What lunch of mine?" he laughed, hiding the bag behind his back. "I haven't got any lunch."

"Oh, come on," she said, taking his arm. "You can eat that stuff of yours tomorrow. How many chances do you get to eat with a babe like me?"

They walked to a small park one block away from the home improvement center. Spreading the contents of the basket on a little table-for-two, Lisa motioned for him to begin.

"Just a sec. Let me say the blessing." Lisa bowed her head as he said a short prayer.

"That was nice," she commented, taking her first

bite of a sandwich. "I wish we had grace at our house."

Bucky picked up a big handful of potato chips and a sandwich. "Boy, this is great." Between bites he began to tell her about work.

"There's so much stuff to keep track of," she said, wrinkling up her nose. "How do you guys ever learn what's what?"

"Well, my dad has lots of that same junk at home, so I sort of know about some of it at least. After that, it's just a matter of learning more and more each day. While I'm workin' I keep my eyes open and try to notice just where everything is. It's kind of fun, really." He popped an olive into his mouth. "Except when it's as hot as this."

"Yeah." Lisa cut an oversized piece of pie and handed it to him. "I feel sorry for those guys working out on the highway in this blazing weather."

All too soon it was time for him to head back for the afternoon shift. Gathering up the trash, he tossed the bundle into a nearby container, then returned and pulled Lisa to her feet.

"Well, thank you again. You are a very gracious young lady."

She giggled. "You're very welcome, kind sir. Anytime at all." As usual, she clung to his shirt sleeve as they walked back toward his workplace.

"Sure would be great to get away from here this weekend and do something fun," Bucky commented suddenly.

"Like what?"

"Oh, I don't know. Just seems like I haven't poked my head out of old Hampton Beach in months." He laughed. "Actually, I don't think I have gone anywhere since some of our baseball road trips." He kicked at a rock. "I mean, day after day, work, go home, sleep, come back and work some more."

"Well, let's go." Lisa was predictably enthusiastic. "Saturday! I'm ready."

Bucky made a face. "I guess I was thinking more about Sunday. You know, church and everything."

She sighed. "Oh, yeah." For a moment she said nothing. "I'm trying to think. Seems like my folks and I are going somewhere Sunday. Oakland for something. Shopping, I guess."

"Well, that's out, then." Bucky grimaced. "I know better than to try to tag along with you on that expedition. I think I'm still off your parents' Christmas list."

"Oh, it's not as bad as that. But, yes, you'd be bored out of your skull shopping with my mom and me. We're the original every-shoe-store-in-the-mall addicts." She gave him a persuasive pinch. "Come on, Saturday's OK, isn't it? You can skip church once a year, can't you? Fifty-one out of 52 isn't that bad."

"I guess not," he responded slowly. "I hate to miss getting a gold star for perfect attendance from Pastor Jensen."

"What gold star?"

"Oh, I'm only kidding." He gave her a sidelong glance. "Sure, let's do it. Where to?"

"It was your idea."

He thought. "Lake Berryessa?"

"Sure!" Then her face fell. "Bucky, how are we gonna get there? Last time I checked, you didn't have a drivers' license yet."

"So what? I bet we could get Sam to go. Then we could gang up on him and force him to drive."

"At gunpoint." She frowned again. "You, me, and him? Isn't that kind of awkward?"

"I was just thinking that," he admitted. He remained silent for a moment. "I know this sounds awful . . . could you fix him up with somebody?"

"Oh, boy," she said with her characteristic silvery laugh. "That does sound bad. But let's see . . ."

As he picked his time card up to punch in, he asked, "Well?"

"I might try Denise."

"Think she'd go?"

"Oh, I imagine. She's very unattached right now. And I know she thinks you're OK."

"Never mind that. What does she think of Sam?"

Lisa shook her head. "I don't know if she even knows him. Don't worry—I'll work on her. You just get Sam and our free car ride lined up."

"OK." Although the thought of skipping church still bothered him, Bucky's pulse flickered at the thought of a day at the lake with Lisa.

"Just a sec." Lisa pulled him closer and landed a resounding kiss on his cheek. "Just so you won't forget me by Saturday."

"Not a chance," he laughed, blushing in spite of himself.

Persuading Sam that evening proved to be a challenge. The older boy was more than reluctant to venture out on a blind date, even with Bucky and Lisa along.

"Who is this girl, Denise, anyway?"

"Oh, you know. That blonde gal who was on the cheerleading squad with Lisa last year. She's real cute . . . and Lisa promised me she'd line her up for you."

Sam groaned. "Oh, brother. Like in the movies.

The poor cousin from Nebraska who can't get a date.''

"Oh, come on. It'll be fun. I'll pay for all the gas.''

"Clear to Berryessa? I hope they've given you a raise at that store you're workin' at.''

"Is it a deal then?''

Sam threw up his hands. "OK already. Just leave me alone!'' He managed a laugh. ''If this doesn't work out, Mr. Stone, I'm gonna dance at your funeral. Your imminent funeral.''

Bucky shook his head. ''No sweat. You'll have a great time.''

His friend grunted an unenthusiastic farewell.

Sabbath morning Bucky did experience a brief moment of turmoil as he watched Mom and Rachel Marie getting ready for church. ''We're just going out for a day in nature,'' he mumbled to himself as he donned blue jeans, pulled an athletic shirt on over his head, and straightened out his slightly mussed hair. It was the same line he had recited—without much success—to his mother the evening before.

During breakfast he kept peeking a glance out the picture window in the living room. Finally he spotted the faded blue Nissan pulling up to the curb. ''Here's Sam,'' he announced, stuffing a last bite of Mom's Sabbath morning fruit toast into his mouth.

His mother forced a smile. ''Have a good time, honey.''

''I will.'' He grabbed his duffel bag and headed out the front door, pausing to tug on Rachel's pigtail. '' 'Bye, kid.''

''Goodbye. Are you going someplace with that girl again?''

''Uh huh.''

"Oh." His little sister gave him a mischievous look. "OK."

Bucky tossed his stuff into the back seat of the little car. "Right on time," he complimented Sam as the pair gunned away.

"Yup." Sam shifted into third gear. "Who do we pick up first?"

"Lisa, of course. I have no idea where Denise lives."

The Vietnamese boy gave his friend a dour look. "I have no idea about her, period. I don't even know who we're talking about here."

"Stop worrying. Would I ever lead you astray?" Pause. "Don't answer that."

Sam laughed. "I say again, if this isn't the greatest day since the Giants beat the Mets in the playoffs last year, I sing at your funeral."

"It's a deal."

Lisa was already waiting out by the curb as they drove up.

Bucky climbed out and let her into the back seat, then climbed in next to her. "To the opera, James, and pray, make haste," he intoned in a clipped British accent.

"Very funny." Sam gave him a mock-poisonous look in the rearview mirror. "Where do we go, Lisa?"

"Just head out to the freeway. Her house is on the way."

"You're sure this is going to go OK?"

"Oh, sure. I fixed it all up." Lisa laughed.

"She really wanted to go with Sam?" Bucky gasped melodramatically.

"No, but I told her I'd do all her homework next

semester, and she finally said OK." Lisa burst into laughter again.

"Funny, funny, funny. Maybe I'll just go to church instead and you 15-year-olds can walk to Berryessa."

"We're only kidding, Sam. Stop worrying!"

A moment later Lisa pointed. "Right here."

Sam wheeled obediently into the cul-de-sac. "Which house?"

"That one . . . with the RV on the side."

Pulling up the driveway, he turned off the engine. "Well, here goes nothing. Wish me luck."

"Good luck, Sam." Bucky and Lisa looked at each other, then grinned. They peered out the window as he rang the doorbell. A moment later the door opened.

"All right, Sam!" Bucky whistled softly as the blonde shut the front door behind her, handing a large picnic lunch box to Sam. The older boy was grinning broadly.

"Stop it!" Lisa pretended to pout.

"Well, Sam doesn't look too heartbroken."

The older boy unlocked the trunk and put Denise's lunch inside before opening the passenger door for her.

"Everybody set?" Sam gave Bucky a wild-eyed look via the rearview mirror, then a broad wink of approval before starting the engine.

Because of traffic, the trip up to Berryessa took just over an hour. The winding mountain roads snaked through the brown California hillsides. One area, showing evidence of a recent brush fire, stretched for miles.

"Remember this? That awful fire last month?" Lisa shook her head in dismay.

"Here we are," Sam interrupted. "Anybody got money for the gate?"

"What gate?" Bucky asked.

"Three dollars. To picnic in here."

Ruefully, Bucky realized he hadn't anticipated this expense. "I think . . ."

"Wait, I guess I got it." Sam found a tattered bill in his jeans pocket. "Remember, Stone, you get the gas bill."

The younger boy nodded gratefully. "Deal."

Several miles down the road they pulled to a stop near the edge of the lake. Two or three ski boats cruised along the other shore, but the area was relatively tranquil.

"This is great!" Denise grinned, hopping out of the car. "I wonder how cold the water is?" She and Sam wandered over to the lake's edge where she stuck an exploratory toe in the water. "Mmmmmm, not bad!"

Bucky turned toward Lisa and lowered his voice. "I guess I didn't plan things very well," he confided.

"What do you mean?"

He hesitated. "Oh, with it being Sabbath."

She raised an eyebrow. "So?"

"Well, like paying for things on Sabbath. To get in here. And now swimming."

"What, don't you go swimming on Sabbath?" Her voice carried no hint of resentment.

He scratched his head a moment. "Stuff like that is hard to answer. I usually try not to do anything so . . . rambunctious, I guess, that I forget what Sabbath's all about."

"Something like, 'Wading yes, swimming no'?"

He gave her a relieved smile. "Yeah, something like that."

"So wade. Who's stopping you?" She kicked off her shoes and gave him her usual mischievous look.

Several hours later Bucky polished off a final handful of celery strips and sighed contentedly. It had turned out to be a good Sabbath after all. Lisa was a genius at deflecting awkward situations, he decided to himself. He sat quietly for the moment, reflecting on just how special she was turning out to be.

"You guys about ready to go?" Sam asked, interrupting his thoughts.

Lisa threw some sand at him. "Already?"

Just outside the park, Sam wheeled into a gas station. "Here's your big moment, Buck."

"Huh?"

"Cough it up, man. Gas money."

Bucky frowned. "We're empty?"

"We only had a quarter tank when we started."

With a sigh Bucky dug into his wallet. Giving Lisa a meaningful glance, he handed Sam a bill.

"Let me out, Denise," Lisa said.

"Oh, right. Me too." Giggling, the two girls headed toward the station's restrooms.

Bucky leaned against the car as Sam pumped away his precious funds. "Well, not bad," the older boy grinned, watching Denise's retreating back.

"See? I told you we'd pick you out a winner. Is the funeral off?"

Laughter. "Sure, I guess." Sam grinned. "Yeah, this was fun." He paused. " 'Course, I did kinda miss church."

The offhand remark caught Bucky by surprise. "You know," he said at last, "I did too. I guess we shouldn't make this a habit."

Sam nodded. "I really like your church, Bucky. And you know, it's helped me a lot, learning about, well, God and stuff."

Bucky considered that for a moment, and then took a breath. "You ought to think about, maybe, Bible studies." He measured his next words. "You know, sort of as a way to get ready to join the church. If that's what you want, anyway."

The other boy studied him. "Seems like you told me that once before." He looked thoughtful, then snapped back to reality as the gas pump clicked off. "What are Bible studies like?"

"Oh, you know, you just study the Bible subject by subject. 'What is God like?' 'Jesus' death on the cross.' 'The Sabbath.' That way you get the big picture." Bucky began to relax. "I'm sure Pastor Jensen would be glad to study with you."

Sam hung up the gas nozzle before responding. For a moment he glanced over to the girls' restroom door. "Where are they?" he mused to himself. Then to Bucky: "No."

The word hung in the air. "What do you mean, no?"

"I don't want to study with the pastor."

"But I . . ."

Sam's eyes twinkled. "I want to study with you."

"What?"

The twinkle faded. "You, Stone. That's it."

CHAPTER THREE

A FREE RIDE HOME

Bucky flipped off the TV set in disgust. "Six in a row! What a cruddy season this is turning out to be!"

His father looked up from the newspaper he was browsing through. "Giants aren't doing so hot, huh?"

"Oh, they're doing wonderful, if you think fourth place is OK."

Dad glanced at a headline before answering. "I guess that happens a lot to championship teams. The next season everything seems to go wrong." He scratched his head. "And, of course, you know every other team in the N.L. is gonna to be going all out to knock the champs off the throne."

"Yeah."

Mr. Stone grinned. "I'll bet it just galls those other teams when the announcer says, 'And now . . . your National League Champion San Francisco Giants.' "

"Yeah, but that hoopla wears a little thin when

you're eight-and-a-half games behind the Reds."

Bucky sighed. Baseball-wise, it was turning out to be a long summer. Not even the All-Star break yet, and the Bay Area boys were fading from contention. "Guess I'll have to switch over to the A's," he muttered to himself as he climbed up the stairs to his room.

Just as he flopped down onto his bed, the phone buzzed. Reaching over, he grabbed the receiver on the second ring. "Hello?"

Sam's voice vibrated over the receiver. "Hey, Buck, what's happening?"

"Oh, nothin'. Just celebrating the extension of the Giants' new streak."

The older boy laughed. "What, seven in a row?"

"Oh, heavens, no. Nothing like that. Just six." He forced a chuckle.

"Are we still on for tomorrow night?"

"Say what?"

"You know, tomorrow night? Didn't you tell me we could start those studies this week?"

"I almost forgot," Bucky confessed. "Yeah, tomorrow's fine."

"What time then?"

"Well, I get off at 5:00," Bucky said after thinking a moment, "and we're usually done eating by about 6:30. Make it 7:00."

"No game on TV tomorrow?"

Bucky laughed. "Well, there is, but I'm too discouraged to think about it."

Thoughtfully Bucky replaced the receiver. Even though he had agreed to study the Bible with Sam several weeks earlier, he hadn't really considered what the promise involved. Wrinkling his forehead in concentration, he tried to recall how his own studies with Mom and Pastor Jensen had gone.

A minute later he padded downstairs to the kitchen. Mrs. Stone was busy making a casserole for Sabbath, assisted by a dough-covered Rachel Marie. "Hi, honey," she greeted. "What's up?"

He sat on the counter. "Remember when we had studies with the pastor?"

She set down her measuring cup. "Sure."

"Did he have lessons for us, or did we just look up verses or what?"

She smiled. "Are you starting with Sam?"

"Uh huh."

"That's great!"

"Yeah, but what do I do?" He paused. "All of a sudden, I haven't got the slightest idea where to start."

As she continued to mix ingredients, she tried to think. "Well, if I remember, Pastor Jensen did have some printed things we worked on together. Kind of a fill-in-the-blank set."

"That's it! OK, I do remember now." He thought for a minute. "Do you think we still have 'em?"

"I imagine." Mom leaned over and pulled Rachel Marie's apron off. "Enough for you, kiddo. Bath time." Then to Bucky: "They're up in my bedroom. I'll get them for you in a minute."

"I wonder if Pastor Jensen has any more sets?"

Mom nodded. "Oh, I'm sure he does. You'd want new ones anyway so you and Sam can fill them in together." She picked up a cloth and began to wipe up. "Why don't you call and ask him? I'm going by the church tomorrow at noon for that ladies' prayer group. I could get them for you then if he has any."

Without climbing down from the counter, Bucky

slid himself over to the wall phone. A moment later, he had Pastor Jensen on the line.

"Oh, Bucky, that's great! Sam wants to have studies with you?"

"Yeah. I tried to talk him out of it—and have him study with you—but no way."

The pastor laughed. "Well, I'll tell you something. He's doing you a great favor."

"What do you mean?" Over the phone he could hear a computer printer clicking away.

"Well, it's like this. I could give him the studies, sure. That's what I do for a living. But if you give 'em, you'll get the benefits that come from that kind of study. Believe me, it's a tremendous learning experience." The pastor's voice softened. "Plus, it's a wonderful thrill to lead someone to Christ. I wouldn't want to take that away from you, Bucky."

The boy was silent for a moment. "I never thought of that."

"And, of course," Pastor Jensen went on, "this will really bond your friendship. Any new Christian needs good, close friends . . . which I know you already are for Sam. But studying together like this will make it a real lasting relationship. You'll see."

"Yeah, I guess."

"Anyway, your mom can pick up a couple of sets tomorrow. That'll be fine."

"Anything in particular I should think about?"

"Huh uh. This set of lessons is really good. You just go through them together, looking up the verses as you go. Of course, any time you can think of personal experiences, that's always good."

"But I don't . . ."

"Oh, you'll be surprised how many things will

come to you right while you're studying. The Holy Spirit almost shouts in your ear sometimes." The pastor chuckled. "You just wait and see."

Bucky nodded to himself. "Well, we'll give it a shot anyway."

Replacing the receiver thoughtfully, Bucky turned to his mother who had been listening quietly. "Well, here goes nothing," he said slowly.

"I was just thinking," she mused, "about that other boy you mentioned to us. During those baseball playoffs of yours. Dan? Is that his name? You told me he was interested, too. Right? Why not a threesome?"

Bucky shook his head. "After that one day in the hallway, we've never discussed it again."

"Oh, really?"

He hopped down from his perch on the counter. "And, boy, after the way this last school year went, I'm not about to go around bringing it up."

A look of concern crossed his mother's face. "I guess it's sometimes best to lay back and wait for something to happen," she said at last. "Still, God just about always works through people. If you don't speak up, maybe no one will."

"Lately, every time I say something, it turns out wrong." He grimaced. "Lisa's dad still thinks I'm some kind of nut."

She put a hand on his arm. "Well, just keep your eyes open for the right chance. If the Holy Spirit gives you your opportunity, then take it!"

He nodded unenthusiastically. "We'll see."

The next morning during his devotions, Bucky spent several extra minutes praying about his appointment with Sam. Then he added as an afterthought, "If I should get the chance, please show me what to say to Dan." He paused. "If anything."

That afternoon work was frantic as the crew
unloaded two huge truckloads of new merchandise.
"Seems like the center must think everybody in town
is planning to spend the whole Fourth of July weekend fixing up their houses," he panted to Gene, a tall
college student who was helping him stock boxes of
hand tools.

"Yeah. Murphy's Law: 'The biggest trucks come
in on the hottest days.' "

Bucky heaved a sigh of relief when the clock on
the wall finally indicated 5:00. "At last!"

Gene took a long drink of water before pulling his
time card out. "What're you doin' tonight?"

Bucky laughed. "You'd never believe it."

"Oh, yeah?"

"A Bible study with a friend of mine."

Gene gave him a curious look. "Huh?"

As Bucky passed the front checkout counter, he
suddenly sucked in his breath. Standing in line, just
getting ready to make a purchase, was Dan.

For a moment he paused. "What, Lord? Is this it?"
As he stood thinking, his pulse quickened.

Just then the older boy spotted him. "Hey, slugger!" His tone was relaxed, friendlier than Bucky
might have expected.

"How ya doin'?"

Dan handed the clerk a bill and accepted his
change. "Great! How's summer been for you?"

Bucky gestured at the huge warehouse. "It's been
all right here, is all." He laughed.

Dan motioned toward the parking lot. "Where ya
headed?"

"Home, I guess."

"Can I give you a ride?"

"Well, I . . ." Almost by reflex, he began to explain that he had his bike outside in the rack. Yet the words died in his throat. "Yeah, that'd be great! If it's no bother."

"Hop in then." Dan nodded toward a gleaming sports car at the far end of the lot.

Bucky eased himself onto the upholstered seat. "Great car!"

Dan grinned. "The payments kill most of my paycheck, but so what?" He turned the key and the engine gunned to life. "This baby is my dream."

As he glanced out the window, Bucky wondered for a minute how he would get to work in the morning. Aloud he said, "How's the job going?"

"Not too bad, I guess. Mostly pumping gas at the full-serve line." Shaking his head, he added, "At these prices, I'm surprised anybody goes for full-serve, but you'd be amazed how many people do. Rich guys off the freeway." He slowed for a red light. "Then some oil changes. Real routine stuff."

Bucky nodded. "You just work a day shift, right?"

"Uh huh. Well, I did do a few graveyards last month when one of the guys was sick. But usually 7:00 to 4:30."

"What are you doing evenings?"

Shaking his head, Dan laughed. "Not a whole lot. Swimming some. Basketball at the gym." He looked at Bucky. "Gearing up for this fall, like I told you?"

Bucky nodded.

"How about you? Anything much?"

"Nah. I see Sam and Lisa every now and then. Not much else."

"Lisa . . . that's the girl you were going out with in the spring?"

"Uh huh."

Dan grinned. "Not bad."

"Yeah."

Bucky hesitated. "Sam's coming over tonight for a . . ." He took a breath. "This sounds dumb: he's comin' over for a Bible study. No big deal, just a casual kind of thing." Carefully he looked over at his friend. "It'd be great if you could come too."

The older boy said nothing. Several long seconds went by. Even with the engine's smooth rumble, the silence hung in the air.

Bucky waited out the long pause. At last, when it appeared his friend wasn't going to respond, he went on, his words slightly rushed. "I remember when you and I talked at school about God and stuff like that. And I've wished since then that we could find another chance to do it again."

Still Dan stared straight ahead as he drove. Finally he turned and looked directly at Bucky. "Listen, man," he said, almost apologetically, "I know what I said. And . . . I . . ." For just a second, Bucky got the feeling a small dam was about to burst. Then Dan turned back to face the road, squinting hard, thinking. "Just not now, OK?"

As they turned the corner onto Woodman Drive, the sporty automobile skidded slightly, veering dangerously close to a parked car at the curb.

"Watch it!" Without meaning to, Bucky yelled.

"Sorry 'bout that," Dan mumbled. He straightened the wheel and slid to a stop in front of Bucky's house. "Right-to-the-door service for a friend." He cocked his head as he looked over at him. "About the other . . . I'll think about it. OK? Just not right now, man."

"Sure. No sweat." *Keep it light!* he told himself as he tugged on the door handle. "Listen, thanks for the ride."

Just as Bucky closed the door, his glance fell on a sack in the back seat. The logo of a nearby convenience store partially hid the six-pack of cans, several of them already opened. Were they soda or beer?

The powerful engine throbbed as Dan wheeled down the street. Bucky stood there thoughtfully, staring at the empty cul-de-sac. "Oh, boy," he muttered to himself before heading into the house.

About 15 minutes before 7:00, he picked up the colorful Bible study guides Mom had brought home. Quickly he scanned the material, looking for any illustration "hooks" he could use.

Promptly at 7:00 the doorbell rang. "Hey, come on in," he greeted his friend.

Sam raised his eyebrows when he noticed the TV set off. "Well, the game's either going great or terrible," he commented.

"Giants are up eleven to two. Goodbye, streak. I figure they can hold that with two innings to go."

"Oh, I don't know," Sam laughed. "These days that might still be rated as a cliffhanger."

"Come on in here," Bucky invited. "We can have the whole family room to ourselves."

Before the two boys began their study, Bucky looked intently at his friend. "I think it's great that you're willing to do this with me," he began. "Is it OK if we start with a prayer?"

His friend nodded.

"Dear Lord," Bucky began, "thank You that Sam

and I are friends and for his interest in You. Please help us as we study to find out the truth about . . . what You're really like." He paused a moment. In the background the wall clock ticked rhythmically. "And, Lord, please be with Dan Litton tonight as well," he continued. "I know he's interested in learning to know You—deep inside anyway. Please give me more chances to help him. Amen."

Sam looked at him with a curious expression, then smiled. "Did you used to pray like that about me?"

"Yeah," Bucky confessed. They both laughed. Bucky handed him a lesson. "Got a Bible?" The older boy shook his head. "Here, I have an extra you can borrow."

The lesson went by quickly. Twice, while Sam was busy penciling in an answer, Bucky marveled to himself how right his pastor had been. God did give examples at just the right moment.

Right at 8:00 Sam filled in the final answer with a flourish of his pencil. "I'm gonna be an A student, man," he grinned.

"Same time next week?"

"Yeah."

"Come on into the kitchen," Bucky suggested. "Let's get something to drink."

"It's still light enough outside for us to shoot some hoops," Sam observed. "Good old Daylight Savings Time."

The two boys spent an amiable 20 minutes tossing free throws through the basketball hoop mounted over the garage door.

Then they had a quick round of one-on-one. "Good move!" Sam grunted as Bucky whistled by him for an easy layup.

"Hey, raw talent!" Bucky replied with a twinkle in his eye.

Finally dusk settled over the neighborhood and they sank down on the front lawn to rest.

"You seen much of Denise lately?" Bucky asked.

Rolling over onto his back, Sam grinned. "This weekend."

"Oh, yeah?"

"Uh huh." He tossed the basketball up into the air, catching it neatly on its downward flight and thrusting it under his head as a pillow. "How about you? Done much with Lisa this week?"

"Nah. She and her family have been off on a trip. Some business her dad had up in Washington."

"She's a great girl."

"You're not kidding." Bucky stared off at the darkening horizon. The growing moonlight eerily outlined the trees in the neighbor's yard. "Boy, this past school year I don't know how I'd have gotten along without her. Or you." He added the last two words with emphasis.

Sam laughed. "Well, she's better looking." He scrambled to his feet. "I gotta go."

"OK." Bucky scooped up the basketball. "See you Sabbath?"

"Yeah. I think so." Sam strolled out to the car and climbed in. "See ya."

Bucky watched the blue Nissan go around the corner. For a moment, his thoughts returned to Lisa. Her perky smile and laugh. Her head resting against his shoulder at church. A tiny smile started to form.

Overhead a dark cloud covered the moon.

CHAPTER FOUR

DIVINE APPOINTMENT AT REGISTER FIVE

July became a blur of long work days, twilight basketball, and Lisa. The young couple found themselves spending more and more time together during the long Bay Area evenings and too-brief weekends.

"You're falling for that girl," Sam teased as they practiced perimeter shots one evening after their weekly Bible study.

"Falling?" Bucky shook his head in mock chagrin. "I'm afraid I'm clean off the cliff."

"Not even 16 and the man is roped down for good." Sam took aim and sent a jump shot swishing through the hoop.

"Look who's talking," Bucky responded. "Every

weekend lately, it's 'Sam and Denise here' and 'Sam and Denise there.' " He picked up the ball and attempted to twirl it on his index finger.

The older boy said nothing, a puzzling expression on his usually cheerful face.

Bucky set down the ball. "Hey, what's wrong?"

The older boy flopped down on the grass. "Oh, nothin', really," he muttered. "It's just . . ."

Bucky joined him on the ground. "What?"

Sam looked at him. "I wonder what Denise thinks about . . . you know, our studying the Bible and church and all that business?"

"Have you talked about it?"

He shook his head. "I'm not like you, man. I can't just bring up things like that the way you do."

Bucky picked up a blade of grass and inspected it in the twilight. "What makes you think it's a problem?"

"Well, not exactly anything. 'Cept I just get the feeling that if she knew anything about it, she wouldn't go for it."

"Does she even know you go to church on Sabbath?"

"Yeah. We were going out and I just told her, you know, 'I'll pick you up after church.' "

"What'd she say?"

"Nothing. Just shrugged and said OK."

"See there? Maybe it's no big deal."

Sam remained unconvinced. "We'll see." He looked off in the distance at the hills on the horizon. " 'Course, when I get baptized, she'll have to know about that."

A tiny thrill went through Bucky as Sam spoke the words *"When I get baptized."* He looked at his friend with genuine fondness. "Well," he said slowly, "you *know* God can take care of it all. I mean, that's the very thing that was in our study tonight. Right?"

"Yeah," the Vietnamese boy answered, forcing a grin. He glanced at his watch. "Man, I gotta go."

Bucky stood and stretched to his full height. With a ferocious leap he slapped the metal basketball hoop with the palm of his hand.

"Wow!" Sam gasped. "How did you do that?"

"Just jump," Bucky shrugged. "Plus I guess I've done a little growing this summer."

"Little nothing!" Sam eyed his friend. "Wow, you're taller than I am now! How much?"

"I don't know. 'Bout six two."

"Wow!" Sam repeated. "Hit it again."

Bucky obliged him with a terrific leap. For a tantalizing second most of his hand perched over the rim of the hoop.

"You got that thing at ten feet?"

"Regulation," Bucky grinned.

"Pretty good," Sam admitted, shaking his head. "Ol' Brayshaw'll be by here with a chocolate cake, ready to make his peace with you." He laughed.

At the mention of Coach Brayshaw, Bucky's face froze. An uncharacteristically hard glint came into his eyes. "No way," he retorted, his voice tense with hostility.

* * *

The next morning Bucky awoke with an unfamiliar sound drumming on his window pane. "You gotta be kidding," he muttered to himself, opening one eye. "Rain? The first week of August?"

He sat up straight in bed and stared out the window. Baffled, he extricated himself from the tangled sheets and headed toward the hallway bathroom.

A few minutes later, he sat down in the corner of his room where he always had his personal devotions, and bowed his head in prayer. Somehow the words in the Bible passage this morning seemed hollow, forced. With a grimace he made himself concentrate.

Finally he had to admit to himself that he knew what was wrong. The emotion from last evening came flooding back as he thought about Sam's chance remark about the high school baseball coach. *Face it,* he lectured himself. *Deep down, you haven't forgiven Brayshaw for what he did to you.*

He winced as he realized the accuracy of his conscience. *In fact, you almost hate him!*

Setting his Bible aside, Bucky sat in the early morning quiet, his mind in turmoil. The rainfall had slowed to a steady drip on his window sill.

All at once he found his angry thoughts being channeled into a quiet but intensely heartfelt prayer. "Why, God?" he breathed. "Why did things turn out this way? How can You blame me for hating old Brayshaw?" He took a deep breath. "I don't want to hate him, but I . . ."

All at once he caught himself. "Yes, I do," he whispered to himself. "I almost like . . ." For the first time he realized how often he had replayed in his mind the scenes from that crucial Friday night game, almost enjoying the opportunity to pity himself —again and again—as the hero in the tragedy.

"Can I forgive him?" he asked aloud. As though a light had suddenly turned on, he realized that forgiving the coach would mean letting go of the resentments he had harbored against him—and even actually enjoyed.

"Please, Lord," he began after a long struggle, "help me to forgive Coach Brayshaw. Right now. Help me to stop thinking about how it made me feel."

For several more minutes he prayed. When he finally opened his eyes he noticed that the sun was beginning to peek through the rain clouds.

* * *

That afternoon he heard his name on the loudspeaker system. "Stone to register five. Stone to register five."

Putting away the box of wrenches he had been sorting, Bucky walked quickly to the front of the warehouse. "Can you take number five for a while?" one of the clerks said. "We're kind of full up here."

"Sure." Several times previously Bucky had manned a cash register during slow periods. With the store's new price scanners, handling a cash register was a piece of cake. He grinned at the opportunity to escape his usual shelf-stocking chores.

Time slipped by quickly. A glance at his watch during a temporary lull showed that he'd been at the new job for nearly an hour.

"I'll take all of these." A familiar sounding voice jerked him back to attention.

"Yes, sir." Without thinking he picked up the first item and ran it over the electronic device. Suddenly he looked up to see who he was talking to. A sharp tingle ran through his whole body.

"Hi, Coach." With great difficulty he forced himself to speak.

The man stood in the narrow aisle with his hands

on his hips. "Mr. Stone." His voice held no hint of feeling.

Bucky fumbled for words, his mind racing. To be face to face with the very person who had haunted his thoughts and now his prayers was an unnerving coincidence. "I . . . I guess I never expected . . ." His mouth felt dry.

Mr. Brayshaw looked him over from head to toe. "No, I don't suppose so." He glanced around to see who was listening. Slowly he turned until he gazed directly at the boy. "Don't think I haven't forgotten about you," he whispered harshly.

His hands trembling slightly, Bucky scooped the four small items into a bag. *Lord, what shall I do?* he pleaded inwardly.

Accepting the man's bill, he set it on the register and pulled out the coach's change. As he handed the coins over, he took a deep breath. "I've been thinking a lot about last year's baseball playoffs," he said softly, his voice unsteady.

A grin twisted the coach's mouth. "Well, well," he said, his voice clipped with terse sarcasm, "we do have something in common after all, Stone."

Bucky breathed a second prayer before speaking again. "I've started to realize how you must have felt," he said at last. "I mean, you didn't know anything at all about my . . . my religion." A pause. There still were no customers in line behind Brayshaw. "And then to be so close to winning the championship . . . I can see now how angry and . . . and . . . frustrated my decision must have made you."

Unexpectedly, the man remained silent, only giving a little nod, almost of sympathy. Bucky's pounding pulse began to slow almost to normal. He felt

God's strength filling him. "I guess I want to say," he concluded slowly, "that for the problems I caused you, I'm really, really sorry." The boy looked him in the eye. "Maybe I could have planned things better, found some better way to tell you what I needed to do. I don't know." For a moment he glanced down, then at the coach again. "I'm really sorry." The last three words were a whisper.

Almost mechanically Coach Brayshaw picked up his bag of supplies. "I, uh . . ." For the first time Bucky could remember, the coach was at a loss for words. There was an awkward silence.

Finally Bucky gave a little cough. "Well, I'll see you later."

"Yeah." Brayshaw moved listlessly toward the front door of the home improvement center. As he opened it with his one free hand, he turned and looked back at Bucky, his eyes questioning.

"Can I help you?" The words almost came automatically as Bucky waited on the next customer, but his mind lingered over the experience of a moment before. *Coincidence? No way!* He breathed a prayer of thanks to God before making change.

Pedaling home later that afternoon he felt a curious sense of relief. Over and over he replayed in his mind the scene at the cash register. *I'm really sorry.* Somehow God had broken through his own resentment and made the apology real. Even as he rode along, he breathed a second prayer, thanking God for creating the "chance meeting" at checkout stand five.

"Maybe I can make it at Hampton High after all," he mused. With the pain of last year's playoffs resolved at last, with Sam's baptism just a few weeks away, and with the nicest girl in high school as his steady friend, maybe life was really worth living.

After supper and a huge plate of strawberry short-cake, Bucky excused himself from the table and went into the other room. Picking up the receiver, he eagerly dialed his seven favorite digits.

"Hello?" Lisa answered on the first ring.

"How's it going?"

She hesitated a second. "OK, I guess." Somehow she sounded strangely subdued.

Bucky frowned. "Anything wrong?"

Lisa gave her little sigh, a habit he'd grown to like. "I . . . I guess I just needed to see you." Pause. "I haven't seen you since Saturday."

Minutes later he pulled up at the driveway leading to the Nichols' home. Sitting on the porch steps was a familiar figure.

"Hi." Bucky left his bike out by the curb and strolled, hands in his jacket pockets, up the sidewalk. "Are you OK?"

Lisa didn't answer. Rising slowly, she reached for his arm. Pulling it out of his pocket, she slipped her hand into his and drew him closer. Slowly the couple began to walk down the street toward a small green-belt area a block away.

Finally Bucky could stand the silence no longer. "Come on now," he teased, his voice light. "Did your dog die or something?"

She turned to face him. Despite the warm evening air, he could feel her shivering. Suddenly she buried her face in his shoulder.

Finally she spoke, her voice muffled by the fabric of his jacket. "We're moving away."

CHAPTER FIVE

JUST ONE LAST WEEK TOGETHER

Bucky's heart froze. For a moment he clutched tighter at the slight form huddled in his arms. "What did you say?" he whispered hoarsely, even though he had clearly heard the words.

Lisa hugged him for several seconds without speaking. Finally she pulled herself loose just a little bit and looked up at him. Her blue eyes were moist.

"We're leaving," she said simply. "Next week. Daddy has a job up in Washington."

Still numb, he led her over to a nearby bench. The young couple sat quietly in the growing darkness. In the distance, just beyond the edge of the park, the street lamps cast soft circles of light. For a fleeting moment, it reminded him of an evening eight months earlier on a bench when he had talked about religion—on a first date!—with her. Suddenly and painfully he realized how much he had grown to care about the girl.

Finally he found his voice. "When did all this happen?"

"Well, several weeks ago." Her voice was strained from emotion. "Remember that trip we took up to Washington a while back?"

"Uh huh."

She slipped her arm through his. "I guess Daddy's company wants him to transfer up there. Run that whole region for his sales division. So he was checking it out."

Bucky's temper flared. "Well, didn't he tell you this was in the works?"

The girl shook her head. "I knew it was business, but, you know, thought he was just handling some stuff for the company. I never imagined it would involve . . . moving." Her voice was forlorn.

They sat in the darkness, thinking. At last he spoke again. "What are we going to do?"

"There's nothing we can do," she responded flatly. "Enjoy each other for one last week."

"One week," Bucky repeated bleakly. Then he sat up straight. "What about school? What about selling your house? All that stuff?"

"The company handles all that," she sighed. "They already have a place for us up there. Near Seattle."

He groaned. "Boy, that sounds like about a million miles away."

"May as well be."

Suddenly he stared at her. For really the first time, he simply looked at her face, memorizing her features—her perky nose, soft lips, damp eyes and cheeks.

"I guess I never have told you," he said reluctantly, "how much it helped me to have you around last school year." Shyly he reached up and touched her cheek. "I don't know how I would have managed without you."

Lisa held his hand tightly. "Yeah," she murmured. Then with a smile: "It was my pleasure."

Suddenly she was in his arms again. "I love you," he murmured softly. It felt strange—but good—to say the words for the first time.

Several minutes went by with neither of them saying a word. A verse from last week's Bible study with Sam flickered through Bucky's mind. "All things work together for good to them that love God." The painful ache in his heart began to subside just a little bit. God had brought her into his life—surely He had a plan that would still bring ultimate happiness to both of them.

Quietly, haltingly at first, and then with growing feeling, the two began to share their deepest thoughts with each other. The darkness of the summer evening enveloped them as conversation drew them together. Bucky realized with a fresh stab of pain how deep emotions and caring ran in her.

Finally they lapsed into silence again. "Guess we're just talked out," Bucky said at last, managing a grin. He glanced at his watch. "Ouch! I gotta get you home."

"What time is it?"

"Almost 10:00."

Lisa stood and held her hand out to him. "Come on."

On an impulse he leaned his tall frame over and gave her a lingering kiss.

"Mmmm. What's that for?"

"Everything." He kissed her again.

She sighed. "The one good thing about good-byes."

"We still have a week," he pointed out.

Lisa was quiet as they walked back toward the house. Suddenly she said, "I wonder what will happen to me with . . . you know, church and everything."

He didn't answer. Several times during the hour on the park bench that same thought had crossed his mind.

"I mean . . . what do you think I should do? I've been going to church with you every Saturday. But up in Washington? I . . ." Her voice trailed off in confusion.

Still Bucky didn't reply. As they reached her front door he turned to face her. "God'll show you what to do."

"Yeah." When she reached out and clutched his jacket sleeve again, he grinned.

"Well, this week we're gonna see a lot of each other," he promised.

"OK." Her voice was a whisper.

* * *

The next day at work he was distracted and listless. The thought of facing a sophomore year at Hampton Beach High without Lisa left him with a sense of overwhelming loneliness.

"Watch it, Stone!" a supervisor barked as Bucky, not watching where he was going, nearly knocked over a display of ceramic flower pots. "And these aren't the parts I asked for. Come on!"

"Sorry." Sheepishly Bucky replaced the box he was carrying and picked up the correct parts. "Hurry up quitting time," he muttered to himself.

With about a half an hour to go, he brightened when a familiar face popped into view in one of the aisles of the paint section. "Hey, Litton!"

"How you makin' out, slugger?" Dan was his characteristically cheerful self.

Bucky hesitated, then replied, "Not so good. I found out last night that Lisa's moving away."

The older boy shook his head sympathetically. "Man, that's too bad. You and her were pretty close, weren't you?"

"Yeah." Bucky nodded. " 'Specially right at the end of last school year, when things fell apart for me. You know, with that game and all. She really stuck with me through all that stuff."

Dan's face was thoughtful. "That was a mess all right. I guess I never really stopped to think how bad it was, especially for you."

"Well, it's over now," Bucky said firmly. "You know how it is. You gotta move on."

"Right." Dan brightened. "An' I know just how you can do that!"

"Oh yeah?"

"Hey, you already know what I'm going to say. Go out for the basketball team this fall?"

Bucky frowned, then forced a laugh. "That's about the third time someone's pitched that at me." He paused. "I'm telling you, there's no way I can play for Hampton High again. Ever."

Dan edged closer. "Listen," he said, "you've got rights just like anybody else at the school. You got as much right as anyone to go out for the team. No matter what happened last year." He looked him over with a quizzical eye. "Plus you've grown about 14 inches in the last two months," he added suddenly. "Boy, how tall are you all of a sudden?"

" 'Bout six two."

The older boy shook his head. "Panthers' JV squad could really use you," he said quietly. "With your size and ability." He scratched his head. "We got a pretty good center in Gorton . . . and I play forward. Chris is a pretty good guard and shooter. But there really isn't a good second forward."

"Who's coaching the JV team this year?"

For the first time Dan hesitated. "Brayshaw."

"What?"

"I know how you feel," Dan nodded uneasily. "But the district cut back funds to Hampton during the summer. Old Brayshaw has to double up baseball and basketball."

"Well, that's it then," Bucky said decisively. "Brayshaw'll pull out a machine gun and empty it on me if I so much as breathe on the door of the gym."

"Yeah, maybe you're right." He sighed and uttered a brief obscenity to himself, then jerked his head up. "Sorry."

Bucky motioned with his hand, indicating that it was OK. "Boy, it would be fun to play, though," he said wistfully.

Dan laughed. "Well, pray about it!" His voice sounded sincere.

"I know you're kidding, but maybe I'll do that." Then Bucky looked at his friend and took a breath. "You thought any more about my little Bible study thing with Sam?"

An uncomfortable expression crossed the other boy's face. "Hey, I've been busy," he retorted, trying to keep his tone light.

"Sure." Bucky glanced at his watch. "Guess I better finish up here."

For a second Dan hesitated, then spoke again. "Look, Buck," he said, almost apologetically. "I know what this religion thing means to you. And that's great." He licked his lips. "But I just don't see it for me."

"How come?"

Dan stood lost in thought for a moment. Then an edge of resentment crept into his voice. "You hear about that TV preacher from Tennessee coming in to Frisco this weekend? Going to 'claim the city for God,' or something dumb like that. Bringing in a bunch of his Bible boys—'prayer warriors'—to drive out all the gays." He mimicked the televangelist's style with sarcastic accuracy. "Man, I can't get into that kind of stuff!" He lowered his eyes. "I mean, what would everybody think?"

When Bucky responded, his voice was understanding. "Yeah." He raised an eyebrow. "I know how you feel."

The statement took the other boy by surprise. "Yeah, I guess you do," he admitted sheepishly. He fumbled in his pocket for his car keys, then looked up with a teasing expression on his face. "Tell you what, Stone. If you play basketball, that gives you another whole season to talk me into this God business."

* * *

That evening for the first time, Lisa sat in on the Bible study with Sam. Bucky had offered to postpone the session, but she had insisted. "Isn't this your last one with him?"

"Well, yeah."

Her old self had returned . . . to a degree. "I don't want you to miss your last session on account of me." A little laugh. "On one condition: you let me come, too."

Bucky had grinned. "Sure!"

Now they sat cross-legged on the floor of his living room, concluding the series of youth lessons. In a way both boys were sorry to see them end.

"Well, this is it," Bucky noted with a smile. "Last question, Sam."

"Yup."

Bucky read it aloud. "Having chosen Jesus as my Lord and Saviour, and recognizing the unique role the Seventh-day Adventist denomination has to play in earth's closing prophetic moments, I have decided to join the Adventist Church, and to demonstrate my commitment through baptism by immersion." He looked over at his friend. "You've been saying yes to everything up till now," he added softly. "What about this?"

Sam had a thoughtful expression. "You know I want to," he responded, his face glowing.

Seated next to Bucky, Lisa stirred. "Hey, I wish I were in on this," she said suddenly.

He looked at her. "I don't know why I didn't include you from the start," he confessed. "We should have all studied together."

"Everything you guys said tonight sounded right to me," she said with conviction. "Why couldn't I just do like Sam here and go for it? Be baptized, too?"

"I . . ."

"I mean, if this means this much to you, that's good enough for me."

Underneath her words something troubled Bucky but he wasn't quite sure what. Surprisingly, it was Sam who spoke up first. "Wait a minute," he said gently. "You haven't studied any of this at all."

"I know, but . . ."

His face grew serious. "There's more to Christianity than just choosing it because someone you like is into it. This whole business of joining Bucky's church is a lot more complicated than I ever realized when I started. There's a lot you don't know—and you need to know it before you jump in."

"Sam's right," Bucky nodded reluctantly. "It was a nice idea, but you really need to read all the fine print first."

Lisa wasn't going to give up that easily. "If I already know I'm going to accept it all, why can't I do my studying afterward?" she demanded.

This time Bucky answered. " 'Cause God wants people to make an *informed* decision about Him. That's why Paul praised the people in Berea so much—they checked out everything he said to them. They didn't just say, 'Well, Paul's a nice guy, let's do it.' "

She slowly nodded. "You're right," she admitted at last. "I wish I weren't moving away next week!"

"Well, I guess we can all agree on that," Bucky sighed. Sam nodded. For a moment the three of them sat there without saying anything.

"When should we aim for a baptism, Sammy?" Bucky broke the silence.

The Vietnamese boy's eyes brightened. "I guess the pastor ought to have a vote," he laughed.

Bucky nodded. "I imagine he'll want to just run over all this real quick with you once more. Just to make sure I didn't feed you any heresy," he chuckled. He punched the date button on his watch. "What do you think? Two or three Sabbaths from now?"

"Hey, no way!" Lisa protested. "This Sabbath. I want to be there, you know."

Bucky gulped. "I . . . I guess we could ask Pastor Jensen."

"Why don't you call him?" Sam sat up eagerly.

Giving them a what-have-you-gotten-me-into look, Bucky went over to the phone. He dialed the number and waited for several rings. A moment later he frowned and raised his eyebrows. "Answering machine," he mouthed to the others. At last he said, "Pastor, this is Bucky Stone, here at home with Sam. I think I have a baptismal candidate for you! Could you please give me a call when you get in? Thanks."

"Well, that's that," Sam commented. "Let me know what you find out." Rising to his feet, he announced, "Guess I better roll." He gave the couple a mischievous look. "You youngsters probably want to be alone."

"Oh, stop that!" Lisa scolded. "I can cuddle up with Bucky here in front of you. See?" She leaned over and squeezed him.

"Yeah, stay awhile," Bucky offered.

"OK." Sam sat back down, kicked off his shoes, and looked over at Lisa. "Sure sorry to hear about you moving away."

She nodded. "Thanks. I'm gonna miss you guys."

They talked comfortably for half an hour. It was nice, Bucky decided, to enjoy some fellowship with both friends at the same time. Somehow it drove the impending separation from his mind.

The ring of the phone interrupted the reverie. "I'll get it," Dad called from upstairs. A moment later: "Bucky? For you."

"Must be Pastor Jensen," Bucky said, scooting himself over to the phone. "Hello?"

"Yes, Brother Stone!" The pastor's cheerful voice filled the line. "What's this about a new member for the church? I don't think we have any room for anyone else."

Bucky laughed. "Right. Well, you're just going to have to squeeze this one in somewhere, 'cause he's special."

"Sam?"

"Uh huh."

"Well, Bucky, that's terrific! You fellows finished your studies? Everything went OK? Sam is comfortable with it?"

"Seems to be." Bucky looked at Sam. "The pastor wants to know if you're really ready for all this."

His friend nodded enthusiastically. "Ask him about Sabbath," he whispered.

Bucky took a deep breath. "I got a big favor to ask," he said into the mouthpiece.

"Shoot."

"We've got our fingers crossed for a baptism this Sabbath."

After a short silence, the pastor said, "Well . . . there must be a reason you boys are in a hurry."

"Yeah, kinda." Quickly Bucky explained about Lisa moving away.

"Oh, dear, that's a shame." The pastor's voice revealed genuine surprise and sympathy. "You two are pretty close, aren't you?"

"Yeah." Bucky was grateful for the darkened living room. Somehow the shadows masked his emotions. Lowering his voice, he added, "She's . . . pretty special to me."

"I know she is, Buck." The pastor's tone was reassuring. "That's tough news to hear." He paused. "But God will work things out. You'll see."

"I know." Bucky looked over at his girlfriend. "About Sabbath?"

"Well, in that case, I don't see why we can't try for it." In the background, Bucky could hear the pastor leafing through some kind of notebook. "We can always make room in our service for a baptism, right? And . . . can Sam drop by for a quick pastoral visit? Or should I come by his house?"

"Oh, I imagine he'll want to come see you," Bucky interjected quickly. He covered the mouthpiece with his hand. "You want to go see Pastor Jensen, Sam, rather than have him stop by your place?"

Sam nodded his head vehemently. "Right!"

"He'll come see you," Bucky explained to the pastor.

"Why don't you let me talk to him?"

"OK." Bucky motioned his friend to the phone. "Here, he wants to talk to you."

As Sam spoke briefly with the pastor, Bucky sat back down next to Lisa. "Boy, this makes me feel a lot better," he commented. "After last night . . ."

"I know." She took his hand. "Life goes on."

CHAPTER SIX

PAINFUL GOODBYE

It was with mixed feelings that Bucky got dressed for church Sabbath morning. On the one hand, Sam's baptism—a moment he had prayed and worked for—had finally arrived. He couldn't help but feel a tingle of excitement about that.

Yet the cloud of Lisa's departure, now just hours away, overshadowed his thoughts. "Our last Sabbath at church together," he muttered to himself as he tugged at the too-short sleeves of his dress shirt.

Because it was Thirteenth Sabbath, the children's divisions were making presentations in the adult Sabbath school. "No story today, Bucky," Mrs. Crawford told him. "I guess you get a day off from being sheriff in the kindergarten department." Gratefully he accepted the extra time to sit with Lisa and Sam in the main sanctuary.

"Hey, you guys," he whispered, sliding into the

pew next to Lisa. She forced a smile and slipped her hand into his.

He looked over at Sam. "All set?"

The older boy nodded. Down at his feet rested a small duffel bag with a change of clothes for after the baptism. His eyes sparkled expectantly despite the fact that he would be baptized without his parents or any other family members present. Only Bucky and Lisa.

"You tricked the pastor into thinking you know it all," Bucky teased in a low whisper. Sam nodded again without a trace of a smile.

All during the Sabbath school program Bucky's mind drifted back to times with Lisa. Their first date at a frosty cold Saturday night school party/dance. Rides home together after Panther victories. Their recent Sabbath trip to Lake Berryessa. Lazy summer evenings sitting in his backyard.

He felt the warmth of her arm against his, the soft skin of her small hand nestled comfortably in his own.

A ripple of laughter interrupted his thoughts. The kindergarten division, dressed up in shepherds' robes, was singing. A little boy standing uncomfortably close to a microphone was steadily three notes higher than the others. Apparently Mrs. Crawford's instructions —"Sing nice and loud, children!"—had made an indelible impression on at least one child's mind.

In spite of himself, Bucky grinned. He leaned over and whispered in Lisa's ear. "Make a note: we must never let Rachel Marie marry that boy."

For the first time the familiar sparkle returned to her eyes. She squeezed his hand. "But what if they really love each other?"

"Yeah, I can relate to that."

She pinched his arm. "You can not. I mean, I know you love me, but I happen to sing like an angel."

At last the moment arrived. Pastor Jensen, dressed in his baptismal robe, gingerly stepped down into the baptistry.

"As Sam is baptized," he began, "I want to invite another young man to come forward. Bucky, would you come on up here?"

Startled, Bucky slipped past Lisa and Mom on his way to the platform.

"For the past year, Bucky has been attending our high school here in town," Pastor Jensen explained. "Now, some of us have wished things might be different . . . but that's how it is at the moment.

"But Bucky, here, decided to make the best of it. In fact, he told me once, 'I'm going to use this as an opportunity to find some young person for the Lord.' "

His voice softened. "Folks, that day has come. Sam Trung Minh is here this morning because Bucky had the courage to share his faith in that high school. In fact, Bucky was the one who gave Sam his Bible studies. If he keeps this up, I may be out of a job here!"

Blushing, Bucky looked up to see a trace of a smile on Sam's face.

"I told Bucky once, 'There's no greater thrill in life than to bring a friend to Christ,' " the pastor continued. "As I look at his face this morning, I can see he's made that discovery as well. Haven't you, Bucky?"

The boy nodded.

The pastor turned to the Vietnamese boy. "Sam, you have a good friend in Buck here." He placed a hand on Sam's shoulder. "But you have an even greater friend in Jesus. And this church family—your church family—rejoices in your decision to serve Him."

He raised a hand in the familiar gesture. "And so, Sam, because you have decided to give your life to Jesus in front of all your friends here, it's my great joy and reward to baptize you in the name of the Father, the Son, and the Holy Spirit." Gently he dipped the tall boy beneath the water.

For a moment Bucky glanced out into the congregation. Lisa, sitting next to Mom, was quietly watching. He couldn't tell for sure: did she dab at her eyes?

After the service, the congregation gathered around to congratulate the new member. Pastor Jensen beamed as the two boys accepted warm greetings from young and old alike.

"Isn't this tremendous?" he said, putting an arm around Bucky. "I can't tell you how much it means to me to have you share your faith this way."

The pastor's face grew more serious as he shook hands with Lisa for the final time. "I understand this is the last time you'll be here for a while," he said softly.

She glanced over at Bucky and then back to the pastor. "I've enjoyed visiting here."

"Well, we will certainly miss you."

The girl nodded without speaking.

"Have you made any plans regarding a church to attend where you'll be living?" the pastor asked in a gentle voice.

"I . . . I just don't know what I'll be doing," she confessed. "I don't even know our new address yet."

He nodded his head in understanding. "Well, when you do, I'd be happy to send along an address of an Adventist church near your home. We'd love to, you know, keep you as part of our great Adventist family."

She hesitated. "I guess . . . I'll have to see how it goes."

"I understand. Well, there's one young man I'm sure will want to stay in touch with you. Just let him know, and I'll do anything I can to help." He gave her a kindly wink.

Together the three friends made their way out to the parking lot. Sam, with his duffel bag in one hand and the pastor's certificate and a new gift Bible in the other, led the way.

"You're sure you want us all for dinner?" he asked.

"Absolutely." Bucky slipped an arm around Lisa. "Last chance."

* * *

The next morning he pedaled over to Lisa's house with a deepening sense of loneliness. All during the past week he had not been able to avoid counting down the days. Five more days . . . four more . . .

And at last the moment of parting had come. Several times during the brief bicycle ride he reminded himself of God's promise to work everything out for good.

As he wheeled to a stop at her home, he saw the family's large auto already loaded to overflowing. Lisa stood on the steps of the house.

"Hi," she greeted him with just a hint of tightness in her voice.

"How's it going?" He motioned toward the loaded car.

"Daddy says we won't be going for about 45 minutes."

"Where's all the rest of your stuff?"

She glanced over her shoulder at the empty house. "Moving van went yesterday." A forced smile. "We slept on the floor last night."

He thrust his hands into his pockets. "One last walk around the block? Think your folks will mind?"

"No, it's OK." Together they headed down the front walkway and up the street. Without speaking, she reached out and held onto his sleeve.

"What do you think will happen with us?" he asked at last.

She looked at him. "I don't know."

"Just play it by ear, I guess," he said slowly.

"Yeah." She moved closer to him. "I love you, Mr. Stone."

It was a memory he would always carry with him. "I love you too," he whispered.

They arrived back at the house just as Lisa's parents were ready to leave. "All set, honey?" Mr. Nichols said as he made one final inspection of the overflowing trunk.

"Uh huh." She clutched at Bucky's arm once more. "I'll call you when I get up there."

"OK." He rested one hand on her shoulder. Mrs. Nichols, already sitting in the front seat with the window rolled up, peered out at them. Bucky leaned over and gave Lisa a last kiss. " 'Bye."

She returned a hug which lingered for only a second, then slipped from his grasp. "Goodbye." Opening the door herself, she squeezed into the tiny space reserved for her in the back seat. Even through the reflection on the window, she had never looked so beautiful.

Gravel under the tires crunched noisily as the

heavily loaded car slowly made its way out to the street. Bucky caught one last glance of her face as the Nichols and their belongings headed toward Interstate 5.

* * *

The next evening Bucky and his father sat wrapped in a huge blanket at the ballpark. "Come on, Buck, just you and me," Dad had urged. "Like in the old days before all the women got their claws into you."

It was a typical Bay Area evening at the stadium —cold! "At least these are great seats," Dad observed as the pair watched the pre-game ceremonies down on the field.

Bucky tried to be cheerful. "Yeah, funny how all sorts of good seats are available when you're in fifth place."

"And now, your National League champion Saaaaaan Francisco Giants," the announcer boomed. It brought a trickle of sardonic applause.

"Guess we won't be hearing that intro much longer," Bucky mused. "Giants may be mathematically eliminated by September 1 the way they're going."

At least this one night things went well. The Giants, apparently sensing that a particular fan needed cheering up, pounded the Phillies mercilessly. Seven runs in the first, three more in the second. A grand slam homer in the fifth brought the tiny crowd to its feet.

"14 to 1!" Bucky grinned, the ache dimming a little bit.

"Feeling better?" Dad asked.

His son nodded. "Yeah, I'll be fine."

Dad took a handful of popcorn. "Well, Lisa won't be the last girl to come along," he commented. "She was a good one, though."

Another inning went by. "You still thinking about playing basketball this fall?"

Bucky shivered as he pulled the blanket closer. "I don't know. Dan keeps telling me I've got a right to try out at least."

"Well, he's right. Coach may keep you off the team if he's bound and determined to be stubborn, but you certainly have a right to show up opening day."

"We'll see." Just at that moment the Giants' left fielder made a spectacular diving grab just inches from the foul line.

"Pretty good catch!" Mr. Stone draped an arm around his son. "That keeps the margin at fifteen runs."

"Who knows? The Giants just might win this game," Bucky replied with a grin.

Two weeks later Bucky's sophomore year began at Hampton Beach High School. Buoyed up by two letters from Lisa and a 45-minute phone call the night before, he pushed through the crowded halls the first day with more ease than the previous year.

The first few weeks of the new school term fell into place uneventfully as Bucky adjusted to the tough tenth-grade schedule. With Lisa gone and with the Panthers' football games on Friday night, he found himself with a suddenly meager social life.

October came and went.

* * *

"There you are!" A hand clapped Bucky on the

shoulder in between classes. "You, sir, are coming with me."

"What?"

Dan Litton poked a finger in Bucky's chest. "Basketball tryouts, JV squad. In ten minutes . . . and I ain't takin' no for an answer."

"But I . . ."

"I said, 'I ain't takin' no for an answer.' " The older boy's face was cheerful and determined all at the same time.

"I did bring my stuff along," Bucky admitted. "I saw the notice about it."

"That's my man!" Dan glanced at his watch. "Hey, let's move it."

Bucky followed him out of the classroom building and across the campus to the large sports complex. "Hurry and suit up," Dan urged. "Old Brayshaw'll be here in a minute."

In the locker area, Bucky nervously slipped into a pair of shorts and basketball shoes. "This'll be the shortest tryout on record," he muttered to his friend.

"Oh, come on. When Brayshaw sees what a big boy you are now, he'll beg for mercy." Dan chuckled, then twisted around, aiming an imaginary jump shot at an imaginary basketball hoop on the wall. "Two!"

A minute later they made their way out onto the main gym floor. The young coach was already taking names of sophomores and juniors milling around a desk. He looked up as Dan approached. "OK, Litton, good to have you." He glanced down at his list and made a mark. "Who's next . . ."

His gaze fell on Bucky. For a moment their eyes locked. A few seconds elapsed before the coach set his clipboard down and took a step forward. "Look,

Stone," he said, his voice low. "Let's keep this quiet, between the two of us." He licked his lips. "Just turn around and walk out of here."

A silence fell over the group. Two boys, dribbling noisily in the corner, picked up the ball and waited expectantly.

"I, uh, I'd like to try out for JV," Bucky said. "Can I at least try out?"

The coach pursed his lips. "You just did." A pause. "And now I'm tellin' you, you didn't make the cut. Sorry." A tiny grin twitched at the corners of his mouth. He picked up his clipboard again.

"Just a minute," Dan interrupted.

Coach Brayshaw glanced over at him. "What is it?"

His voice steady, Dan said, "Stone, here, deserves a tryout just like anybody else here. If he don't measure up, fine." He took a breath. "But you can't just wave your hand and make him disappear."

"Says who?"

Dan's face flushed. "Says me," he responded, his voice low but even.

The coach said nothing for a moment. His face held a question mark.

When Dan saw no response forthcoming, he took a step forward. "You either give Bucky a legitimate tryout, or I guess you can do without both of us this season."

"Dan!" Bucky nudged his friend. "No way! I won't let you do that!"

"You stay out of this," the older boy growled. He turned back to the coach. "Bucky played his guts out for your ball team last season, and you know it. Panthers wouldn't even have been in the playoffs without him. Then when he did what he had to do, you booted him." Dan was breathing heavily now. "Well, now I'm doin' what I have to do."

Coach Brayshaw looked around nervously. "Then what do we do when there's another game on Friday night? Has Stone, here, switched churches during the summer?" he sneered.

"Then you work it out!" His voice was forceful now. "You're the coach. Jewish boys have the exact same problem. If one of them was talented enough, you wouldn't hesitate to change the schedule. You can make arrangements so a student in this school can play without tossing his religious beliefs in the trash can. Can't you?" He matched the coach's belligerent tone.

"What about the playoffs?"

Dan looked at the coach evenly. "If Stone and I don't play, I don't think you'll even have to worry about that. If we do, then you'll work that out, too. That's your job."

The athletic director said nothing for a moment as he looked around at the other boys, measuring their mood. The silence was electric. Finally he spoke again, but this time his tone was more subdued. "I'll tell you what. We'll have our tryouts." A pause. "Stone, too. Then I'll pick my team. My team, Mr. Litton. If Stone happens to make the cut, then the rest of the team is going to vote. Every man on the team will vote whether to let Stone play again . . . after what he did to us last year."

Dan pondered it for a moment, then looked over at Bucky, who gave him a slight nod. "OK. Just remember, I get a vote too." His eyes scanned the gym, probing the gaze of his fellow teammates.

CHAPTER SEVEN

THE BLUFF
WORKS TWICE

"Come on, ring!"

Bucky paced back and forth in the living room near the phone. For the third time in the last ten minutes he glanced at his watch. "Team meeting oughta be over by now!" he growled impatiently.

Finally he forced himself to sit down on the couch. Leaning back against the overstuffed cushions, he thought once again about the previous day's bout with Mr. Brayshaw.

Even now he couldn't get over the face-to-face showdown between the athletic coach and Dan Litton. Litton's bold challenge still rang in his ears: "You either give Bucky a legitimate tryout, or I guess you can do without both of us this season."

Had he been bluffing? Bucky wondered.

"Tryouts in five minutes!" the coach had snapped. Bucky had had just enough time to grab a quick drink of water and breathe a frantic prayer of supplication. "Please, Lord, help me to do my best. For *Your sake!* Please!" As he stepped to the line for the first test he had resolved that—come what may during the season—he would never again let God down.

Now a day later, Bucky's heart flooded with gratitude as he considered how God had answered his prayer.

"Mom, everything clicked!" he had exclaimed, sitting in his basketball clothes on the kitchen floor an hour later. "Free throws: eight for ten. Perimeter shots, four out of seven. Dribble routines—I think I handled them as well as anybody there." He paused. "And I'm as tall as anybody except Andrew Gorton, the center."

Dan had confided as they left the athletic building after the game that they would have to name Bucky to the squad. "There's no way he could put you off now," he observed, shaking his head. "Man, you really nailed that tryout!"

Still flushed with excitement, Bucky had actually dared to hope. "But what about that vote?"

The older boy shook his head. "We'll see," he said carefully. "A couple of those guys were on the baseball squad last May, and I know for a fact they're still mad at you."

Now Bucky waited for the phone to ring. "Come on . . ."

At that very moment, it did. Scooping up the receiver on the first ring, he blurted, "Well?"

On the other end Dan laughed. "How'd you

know for sure it was me?''

He's laughing. That must be good! Bucky thought. ''Come on, I been sittin' by this silly phone waiting for the last half hour. Tell me what happened.''

''Well,'' Dan began slowly, ''I guess I don't know how to tell you this . . .'' A painful pause. ''I'm afraid you're gonna have to play ball with me this year!''

''All right!'' Bucky raised a fist in celebration. ''You did it, man!''

Dan laughed again. ''My bill's in the mail.''

''Hey, I'll pay it. I really owe you one.''

''Well, I'll tell you, you kinda do.''

''What happened?''

''Well, Coach called us together. And of course you know he wasn't going to make any great speeches in your favor. He just kind of said, 'You know the score, men. Yes or no?' ''

''Then what?''

There was a short silence. ''I gotta tell you, from the looks on everyone's faces, it didn't look too good.''

''Really?''

Dan said something unintelligible to someone on the other end, then continued, ''Yeah, Gorton and one or two others acted like they really wanted to shoot you down.''

''Well, what happened?''

The older boy chuckled. ''Well, I figured, you roll the dice once, you may as well roll 'em twice. I just stood up and announced, 'What I said earlier still goes. You guys vote Stone in or you do without us both.' ''

For a moment Bucky could find no words to

express his thanks. "That did it, huh?" he managed at last.

"Yeah." Dan coughed, embarrassed. "You're in . . . by the hair on your chin, my man."

Bucky sighed in relief.

"And there's just one more thing."

"What's that?"

Dan took a deep breath. "You and I have got to deliver," he said softly. "That's all there is to it." He paused. "We are out on a limb, and we just gotta make sure we don't get sawed off. 'Litton and Stone Come Through in the Clutch' is going to have to be a pretty steady headline in the paper."

"You got it. And Dan . . . thanks."

* * *

The next afternoon at practice he suited up nervously in the locker area. An air of tension mingled with the odor of sweaty socks and used towels. Several athletes standing nearby clustered with their back to Bucky, engrossed in conversation. Lacing up his basketball shoes, he stood up straight, stretching to his full six foot two.

Walking over to where Andy Gorton, the lanky center, was slipping on his jersey, Bucky offered his hand. "Thanks for letting me play," he began. "I'll do all I can to help the team . . ."

Gorton stared at the outstretched hand, then turned his back on him and wandered off.

A sense of dread filled Bucky's heart. Was it going to be like this all year?

Please, God, help me to break down these walls! he pleaded as he took his place in line. Coach Brayshaw took roll, his voice even as he called out Bucky's last name.

"Calisthenics," he announced without fanfare. Quickly he led the squad in a short but grueling series of exercises. Bucky, who had kept in shape through-out the summer, managed to finish the set without much strain. Several of the boys, he noticed, were almost gasping for breath at the finish.

"Some of you girls act like you spent all summer gorging yourselves at Dunkin Donuts," the coach snapped. "Come on!" He gave several a hard look. "Get yourselves in shape or you'll be buckin' for a spot on the frosh squad."

For the next hour he ran everybody through drills: layups, passing exercises, one-on-one full court, set-ting screens for shooters. Bucky had to admit that Coach Brayshaw knew his stuff. "I thought he was just baseball," he whispered to Dan during a short break. "How'd he get so good at basketball?"

Dan grinned. "He's no dummy."

The last fifteen minutes was a practice game, Red on Blue. Bucky and Dan, both assigned to the Red squad, played furiously, but it was a ragged perfor-mance. Passes consistently went awry and too many players, Bucky noted, had a "get-the-ball-and-shoot" mentality. He mentioned it to Dan on their way out of the sports complex after showering.

"Yeah, these guys don't seem to know that a good pass is about the best way to a sure score. Some of 'em, the minute the ball lands in their hands, heave it up toward the basket, even if they're 20 feet out." He snorted.

"You did OK in there," Bucky offered.

"Thanks." Dan shielded his eyes from the late afternoon sun. He looked over at Bucky. "I been thinking . . ." he began slowly.

"What?"

"Just 'cause Coach got stuck with puttin' you on the team doesn't mean he's ever going to play you."

Bucky sucked in his breath. "You mean he might . . ."

The other boy nodded. "Yeah, just let you rot on the bench. That'd be perfect revenge for him."

Inside Bucky could feel a slow rage beginning to build. "I . . . I never thought of that. You know, that's what he'll do!" He slammed his fist into his other hand. "Man!"

His teammate said nothing for a moment.

"What can I do?"

Dan's face was thoughtful. " 'Course you don't know that's what he'll do."

"Oh, he will," Bucky interjected dourly. "Anybody would. It makes perfect sense."

"Yeah." Dan's athletic bag brushed against his leg at every step as if it had something heavy in it. Finally he spoke again. "I'll tell you what." He paused. "You and I just have to team up in practice and do so well he'll have to use us together."

Bucky frowned. "What do you mean?"

"I mean, get together, work out some slick two-man plays. Every time we scrimmage, we pull 'em out of our hats. If Coach sees you and me pulling off enough razzle-dazzle in practice, when we're in a close game, he'll know that's his only salvation. Litton/Stone!"

"Do you think it'll work?"

"I don't know what else you can do." Dan chuckled. " 'Cept kill him!"

"I'm sorry, my weird religion won't allow it," Bucky said, forcing a laugh.

Dan cracked up. "Yeah, I figured that."

* * *

The next Sunday Dan came over to Bucky's place and the two spent an exhausting hour and a half together. Dan was brimming with clever plays, Bucky noted.

"Now take the standard give-and-go," Dan explained at one point. "Textbook NBA play—except that high school teams botch it all the time."

"Like how?"

"Say you're bringing the ball down the left side," Dan explained. "I line up along the left side of the key. 'Bout here." He took his place. "Now, I got a defender right behind me, and you got a guy in your face. Right? Now, on the give-and-go, you stop, bringing your man to you. Then pass the ball to me and *break* around your man for the basket! I feed it right back to you."

"So what's so hard 'bout that?"

Dan picked up the ball. "Well, first of all, you got to get past your man. Feed me the ball, then, boom! You blow by him. One quick step and you have 'im beat.

"Then I got to fake my guy out, like I'm going to drive off to my right and shoot," Dan continued. "That gets him out of the way and leaves you wide open to the hoop.

"Or I can do this. You feed me, I'll fake a pass off to my left, then hand you the ball when you blow by on my right side. Your left side." He motioned.

Bucky looked confused.

"Here." Dan tossed him the ball. "We'll do it in slow motion."

As Bucky came down the driveway on the left

side, Dan said, "There. Get about six feet away from me and then stop. Look around—kind of leisurely —for someone to pass to." He went through the motions. "OK, now pass it to me quick and then shoot by me on the left. I'll fake the other way."

Bucky complied. With an easy toss, he then darted by an imaginary defender. Just as he passed Dan, the ball appeared out of nowhere and into Bucky's hands. With an easy two steps, he laid the ball in off the backboard.

"See how that fake the other way will confuse the other team?" Dan beamed.

"Yeah, it almost confused me!" Bucky confessed.

"Now, of course, we can run it both ways," Dan said enthusiastically. "I can also fake right and then feed you coming on my left. You then charge right down the middle of the lane for a layup."

Bucky shook his head in confusion. "How will I know which way we're going?"

"Watch my eyes. Just before the pass-off, I'll give a little move which way we're going. Try it."

Again Bucky charged up the driveway. This time Dan gave the tiniest glance to his left. As Bucky passed it in he surged forward and took the pass into the center of the lane. Leaping high in the air, he dropped the ball into the hoop.

"Man, you can almost slam it!" Dan grinned.

"I see how that signal works," the younger boy admitted. "And, you know, we can run that both ways. I can feed it to you too."

Over and over the two boys worked the play. Slowly but steadily their timing improved until they could run it from either side of the basket, left or right, without a hitch.

Finally Bucky signaled "enough!" Gratefully the pair sank down on the grass. "Man, you sure know your stuff!" he grinned.

"When you're not any taller than I am," Dan said, "you got to make up for it by being a sneak!"

Bucky lifted himself up on one elbow. "I still don't see myself gettin' much playing time," he said slowly. "With Coach bein' down on me . . . plus all the team too."

"I've been thinking about that some more. I think I have an idea."

"Lay it on me."

"Well," Dan said, pulling a blade of grass out of his hair, "you've seen what a lousy passing team we are."

Bucky laughed. "Really."

"All these guys love to score," Dan went on. "And if they get enough assists from a guy named Stone, sooner or later they're gonna start likin' him a whole lot more than they do right now."

"You mean . . ."

Dan picked up the ball. "You, sir, are going to become the Magic Johnson assist champ of the whole league." He tossed the ball to his friend. "You feed old Gorton enough easy hoops under the basket, he'll come around."

"Boy, I hope so." From his prone position, he took careful aim at the hoop high overhead. With a nonchalant toss, he flipped the ball up and it clanged off the rim. He grinned. "You sure I can't shoot it myself at least once in a while?"

CHAPTER EIGHT

A FRANTIC
COMEBACK

Loud music throbbed across the quadrangle as students at Hampton High had lunch. Sam and Bucky sat at the edge of a lunch table on the far side away from the ever-occupied basketball courts. Even after his grueling one-on-one session with Dan the previous day, Bucky's pulse quickened as he watched the furious action.

"Can you keep up with those guys?" Sam teased.

Bucky snapped a long carrot strip in half and popped one into his mouth before answering. "Oh, I dunno. Those are varsity guys."

"How's the JV team look?"

Bucky made a slight face. "Just fair, if you want to know the truth." He paused to watch a senior drive past his defender for a quick layup. "Foul on that one," he muttered. Then to Sam: "Most of the guys on JV are shot-happy. Almost no passing ability."

"Well, hope you guys do OK."

Bucky munched at a huge chocolate brownie without responding. Just then a knot of cheerleaders trooped by the rusted metal picnic table. Even in the cold November air they wore their brief outfits. For a moment he thought back to the previous school year. During most of second semester he had often had lunch with Lisa. Her vivacious chatter had made the time flash by. A wince of loneliness tugged at him.

A glance at his watch told him it was nearly time for geometry. "Well, I got a test on all of chapter 5," he said dourly. "Better move out."

Sam waved him off, taking a last swig of soda as he did so. "Good luck on the test. And good luck with practice this afternoon."

* * *

As Bucky suited up for scrimmage, he glanced over at Dan. As a tiny grin crossed his face, he slithered along the bench to the older boy. "Don't forget our signals," he muttered out of the corner of his mouth.

After the routine number of pushups and laps, Coach Brayshaw divided up the squad once again. "Red, Blue, here we go. Let's see what we can get done in 20 minutes."

Bucky raised an eyebrow. It was the first time he, Dan, and the tall center, Andy Gorton, had been assigned to the same squad. Brayshaw tossed the ball up and Andy easily controlled the tip, deflecting the ball toward Dan. Catching Bucky's eye, Dan began dribbling up the floor.

Moving quickly to the side lane mark, Bucky

stationed himself with his back to the basket. Behind him was a blue-shirted defender. As Dan dribbled closer, Bucky gave an almost imperceptible eye motion toward the center of the lane. Dan, guarded tightly by another Blue defender, stopped dribbling and looked around as if to spot an open man. With a quick lob toss, he sent the ball right into Bucky's hands. A split second later he dashed past his defender and right toward Bucky, who faked left and then smoothly laid the ball back in Dan's hands for an unopposed drive for a layup. Score!

A groan went up from the Blue squad. "Somebody pick him up!" growled the backup center.

Bucky and Dan scurried back to play defense. "Not bad!" Dan whispered, giving Bucky a quick high five.

A few plays later, with Red already up by six points, Bucky dribbled down the court. Picked up by a defender, he passed the ball off and then moved over to the low post near the basket. Moments later, the ball handler, surrounded by two defenders, tossed in desperation back to Bucky, who was still tightly hemmed in by one of the Blue guards.

"Shoot it!" a Red player hollered from midcourt. Indeed, it was the very situation that too often led to a wild, low-percentage shot. But Bucky held the ball for a moment, his eyes scanning the floor. Standing motionless at the top of the key, Andy Gorton waited for him to take a shot. With a quick bob of his head, Bucky motioned to the center: *Down the middle!*

Startled, the center took a few steps forward. Whirling quickly, Bucky passed the ball deftly into Gorton's hands, who caught it and laid it in, all in one

motion. Grinning, Bucky headed back down the court
to play defense.

"Nice pass," the center muttered grudgingly as he
took his own post under the opposing basket.

"Pretty move, Gorton!" the coach hollered over
the clatter of the ten players traveling the length of the
court. "Way to move in!" A pause. "Good assist,
Stone," he added after a slight pause.

Twice more during the brief practice game Bucky
and Dan worked the give-and-go to perfection. And
Bucky proved to be an uncanny passer, finding Andy
and Dan open for easy layups or short jump shots. Just
once one of his passes eluded the tall center, who
simply wasn't paying attention.

"Guess I gotta keep my eyes open when you've
got the ball," Andy panted with a grin as they trotted
back up the floor. His dark skin glistened with perspiration. "My fault on that one, man." He slapped
Bucky on the back. "Just keep 'em coming."

Bucky breathed a prayer of thanks as he showered
off after the game. "Maybe the guys'll warm up after
all," he thought to himself. "Dan was right about
good passing making points . . . and not just basketball points, either!" He rode home with a cautious
smile on his face.

The next morning Bucky enjoyed a few extra
minutes basking in the hot shower. The warm streams
of water beat down on his head and shoulders as he
stood motionless, thinking about the upcoming game.

"Wonder if Coach'll put me in," he muttered to
himself as he toweled off. He added a short "Thy will
be done" postscript to his morning prayer before
heading down to breakfast.

"Tonight's it, huh?" Dad took a bite of cornflakes

and glanced over at his son.

"Yeah." Bucky crossed his fingers on both hands. "Wish me luck."

"Do you think Mr. Brayshaw will play you?" Mom forked a second biscuit onto Rachel Marie's plate with a smile.

"I don't know," he responded slowly. "Things went real good in practice, but I know he still wants to 'get' me."

* * *

The gymnasium was already filling as Bucky donned his new junior varsity outfit for that evening's game with the Cougars. Hampton High had a reputation for loyalty. Even JV games drew large crowds of vocal community fans. Posters and homemade signs dotted the walls, while two solitary championship banners proclaimed Panther triumphs in '85 and '86.

"First game, men," Coach Brayshaw had warned, "is a big one for us. Let's get off to a fast start! 1 and 0 after tonight!"

The murmur of support was strangely subdued. Bucky listened intently for the names of the starting five players.

"Gorton at center." The coach gave his tall star an encouraging nod. "Need a huge game out of you, big guy." He looked down at his list. "Litton, White, forwards, . . ."

The selection did not surprise Bucky. Before the two athletes even suited up, he had confided to Dan, "He ain't gonna do it."

Still, he resolved now to be an enthusiastic part of the team. "Win! Win! Win!" he barked with the rest of the squad as they huddled together for a group cheer.

A smattering of cheers went up from the stands as the athletes trotted onto the floor. "Go! Go! Panthers! Go! Go! Panthers!" A string of cheerleaders began to whip the student body into a burst of excitement.

The game got underway with the usual mix of JV confusion. Even with days of practice and endless drills, the games themselves invariably descended into an undisciplined playground contest.

"Pass off!" Coach Brayshaw hollered from the bench as a Panther forward tried a shot from more than 20 feet away. "Work it around!"

The two referees called fouls meticulously and the frequent pauses in the game gave both coaches opportunity to shuttle fresh players in. Several times Coach Brayshaw looked right through Bucky and then selected another squad member to play.

During halftime in the locker room, Bucky slid over to Dan. "How's it goin' out there?"

The older boy grimaced. "Well, you're watchin' it all," he growled. "No passin', no plays. Just run and gun." He gave Bucky a sympathetic look. "Sorry about how Coach is treatin' you."

"Well, no surprises there," Bucky replied, trying to keep his voice light. "Get a few assists for me."

During the second half the visiting Cougars began to slowly pull away. The red-clad squad had a slight height advantage that was finally taking its toll. Also, their crisp passes and ball movement were leading to easy baskets despite the Panthers' frenetic defense.

Coach Brayshaw signaled that he wanted a time out, and Andy Gorton caught the referee's attention. Reluctantly, the white-uniformed home team headed for the sideline.

"Tighten up!" Coach Brayshaw repeated over and

over. "And get that forward of theirs. He's eatin' us alive!"

For several minutes afterward it appeared the Panthers might rally. Two quick jumpers by Dan brought the crowd to its feet—Panthers down only by 7! But a three-point bomb and a devastating fast break put the Cougars up by a hefty 12 once again with only 5 minutes left.

The referee's whistle brought another halt to the play. "Two shots on the foul, number 14." The official motioned for Litton to take his place at the free throw line.

"Sub!" Brayshaw's voice was unexpected.

Bucky looked up. Coach was staring right at him!

"Go in for Walters, Stone," Brayshaw commanded. He gave Bucky a long, meaningful look.

His heart pounding, Buck bounced on to the court. "Thanks," he murmured to the coach.

He sidled up to Dan. "Get these two and let's go to work!" Quietly he sent up a prayer. *Help me to do my best!*

After taking a deep breath, Dan swished the first shot through the net. A hopeful cheer swept the building. "One more!" Bucky urged. Dan took careful aim. Swish!

The Panthers held the opposing squad scoreless the next time. Taking the rebound, Dan headed cautiously upcourt. The defenders were back en masse. Bucky caught Dan's eye as he approached, dribbling expertly. Quickly he moved to his usual spot near the lane.

The quick lob toss, head fake, and dash to the basket worked to perfection. Pounding hard, Dan laid the ball gently off the glass for two more points. Down by 8! A roar filled the building.

"Hold 'em now!" Bucky breathed at Andy Gorton, the sweat-drenched center. Flanked now by Dan and Bucky, the tall, lanky player had a new look of intensity.

A moment later a second cheer went up as Andy blocked a shot—right into the hands of a teammate. "In your face! In your face!" the cheerleaders chanted as the fast-break points made the deficit a scant 6.

"Time out!" The Cougars huddled near their bench, trying to figure out a plan to stop the revitalized home team.

Bucky edged over to the center. "Let's run one down the middle. Like in practice, remember?" He turned to Dan. "Try to set a pick for him if you can."

Once again the Panthers' swarming defense held the other team's shooters, but now the time clock showed just two minutes left. Bucky took the rebound from Andy and passed off to a guard who headed up the left side of the floor. Dribbling near the end line, he flipped it back to Bucky, who looked over to Dan, near the top of the key. Standing next to him was the expectant Andy.

"Now!" Bucky tossed the basketball to Dan, who faked once and then sent it right back. Almost instinctively the center whirled to his left and charged down the center lane. His defender turned to follow, but found a bulky Dan Litton directly in his path. Bucky shoveled the assist pass to Andy, who drove for a layup. A whistle pierced the air. Cougars 72, Panthers 68!

"A foul, too?" Bucky gasped. "All right!"

Andy stood at the free throw line, sweat dripping from his forehead. "Come on!" Bucky urged.

"One shot. Play the miss, fellas," the referee advised. Andy sighted carefully—it was a huge free throw.

"Score!" The cheerleaders directed the crowd in a chant. "Beat those Cougars! Beat those Cougars!" The ball rattled through the hoop. A second later the chant switched: "DE-fense!" Thump thump! "DE-fense!" Thump thump! A quick glance at the clock showed 1:17 to go.

At the other end, Bucky took a desperate chance, straying far out of his territory to harass an enemy shooter. "Pick up my man!" he hollered over his shoulder as he leaped high in the air, trying to block the guard's shot. Another cheer went up as the ball bounced off the rim and into Dan's hands.

The star forward caught Bucky's eye as the team moved downcourt. *One more time?* Again the give-and-go worked to perfection, as Dan lumbered up the key after receiving Bucky's pass.

"This is it!" Dan gasped to Bucky as they backpedaled furiously for a last stand. "Down by one!"

The Cougars handled the ball methodically, working the 45-second shot clock to perfection. With just seconds left, their top guard let fly with an outside bomb. The crowd sucked in its breath. Straight as a string . . . but just an inch too long! Another roar went up as the ball bounced high in the air and a leaping Andy Gorton snagged it.

Time out! Over in the corner of the gymnasium, a small knot of band students played a brass fanfare. The white-clad Panthers sat on their bench. Coach Brayshaw's eyes intensely scanned them. "One more chance, guys," he hissed eagerly.

Dan took a deep breath and wiped his forehead. "I got a play," he said. "Buck and I been working on it. A fake-shot lob pass that I think'll work."

"How's it go?" a guard wanted to know.

Dan pointed with his finger. "We crowd the left side, draw their defenders over that way, 'specially their forward. Except for Bucky. He heads out to the right." Pausing, he looked over at the other team's bench. "I come up, count down the clock. With about 8 to go, still maybe 25 feet, I let one go. Everybody figures it's a long bomb." Eagerly he looked around. "Except that right when I start the shot, Buck breaks for the basket. It's a pass instead. Right into Stone's hands. He lays it in, we win."

"What in the world is that?" Brayshaw demanded. "Have you practiced it?"

"We just worked it up," Dan explained.

"I don't know," the coach muttered reluctantly. "Seems like we ought to go with Andy for a last shot here. What if you hit the rim?"

"Hey, Coach, Bucky here hasn't taken a shot all night," Andy put in. "He's been passing so much no one will expect it. I say go for it."

Dan shot the center a thankful look. "Up to you, Coach." The gymnasium buzzer sounded harshly.

Brayshaw shook his head doubtfully. "We're out of time." As he peered up at the clock, a frantic expression in his eyes, he said something under his breath. "OK, Litton, I hope you know what you're doin'!"

The team returned to the floor. In the corner a last "Charge!" fanfare went up from the horns. The crowd, by now exhausted, tensed for a final 20-second showdown.

Taking the ball from the referee, Dan passed it to Andy, who fed it right back and made his way over to the left side of the court. The other players, scurrying in a seemingly haphazard manner, also flooded the left side.

Bucky, trying hard to slow the pounding in his chest, settled on the right side of the court. "Come on, Dan, make that lob good!" he pleaded to himself.

With 10 seconds to play, Dan slowed his dribble. The defending guard edged toward him hesitantly, but gave him a few feet of room. They were still too far away for in-your-face defending.

Suddenly the crowd gasped as Dan took sight of the basket. "Not yet!" Coach Brayshaw yelled as a decoy. Quickly bolting past his defender, Dan, pretending not to hear, took aim and let a long 28-footer fly. The crowd, rooting with its hearts for a basket, groaned as the ball sailed wide of its mark . . . and right into Bucky's grasp. The Cougars' center whirled in desperation and leaped toward him, but hours of practice paid off for Bucky. With a quick release, he eased the ball back up, off the backboard, and neatly into the hoop just as the final buzzer sounded.

CHAPTER NINE

MEETING IN COACH BRAYSHAW'S OFFICE

The gym exploded as the winning two points flashed up on the huge scoreboard. Panthers 73, Visitors 72!

Grinning from ear to ear, Bucky gave Dan a huge bear hug. "What a perfect pass!" he shouted. "Right on the money!" The rest of the team piled around, pounding them on the back. Coach Brayshaw stood staring at them, a strange expression on his face.

Along the sideline an impromptu chant went up from the string of cheerleaders. "Dan and Bucky —ain't we lucky! Dan and Bucky—ain't we lucky!"

Sweaty but flushed with victory, Dan stepped forward and gave the coach a victorious high five. "Where's the tub of Gatorade?" he hollered to the team. "Let's give this man a bath!"

"No way!" Brayshaw protested with a grin. "I got my best duds on!" He punched Dan lightly on the arm. "I gotta admit, that was slick. And your lob was perfect. Nice goin'!" For a moment his eyes fell on Bucky.

Bucky tensed, waiting. Suddenly the slowly diminishing roar of the cheering fans faded into the background. The coach licked his lips, his composure suddenly shaken.

Forcing a smile, Bucky took a step forward. "Great job, Coach!" he said. "Way to go."

"Yeah," Mr. Brayshaw managed at last. As he gave Bucky a long look, his eyes still held a trace of torment. Finally he held out his hand. "Nice game," he muttered.

The awkward moment passed as quickly as it had risen. "To the champagne!" Andy hollered. A cheer went up from the squad.

"No champagne," the athletic director retorted, now smiling again. "It's just one game. We're 1 and 0."

"Hey, we ain't gonna win a monster squeaker like that one for a long time," the tall center responded, raising both fists high in the air. The glowing knot of athletes headed for the corridor leading to the showers.

As Bucky passed by the scoring table on his way out, something in the stands caught his eye. A tall, blonde girl standing alone in the fourth row stared at him, a curious smile on her face and frank interest in her eyes.

His pulse quickened. Afraid to meet her gaze, he averted his own eyes and looked over at Dan. "Who is that?" he hissed under his breath.

Dan shook his head with a grin. "I don't know," he responded softly. "But I'll bet you're gonna find out! And you'd better not write Lisa about her, either."

Embarrassed, Bucky punched Dan on the shoulder. Afterward he showered quickly, toweling off his short-cropped blond hair. "Didn't you say your folks came tonight?" Dan asked.

"Yeah." Bucky tossed the damp towel into a bin. "How about yours?"

"Naaah." Dan slipped his expensive watch onto his wrist. "I'm on my own tonight, and, boy, am I gonna party!"

A warning bell sounded in Bucky's mind. He gave his friend a probing look. "Go easy," he advised.

"Hey, don't worry. I know my limit on beers." A short laugh. "I can count to 20!"

Bucky swallowed hard. "Well, just . . ." He left the thought unfinished.

"See ya after Thanksgiving vacation, slugger," Dan tossed over his shoulder. "December we really start to play . . . two a week, baby." He swaggered out into the night.

A moment later Bucky followed. Over by the parking lot stood his parents, Rachel Marie holding hands with Mom.

Suddenly he heard a voice coming from his left. "Great game, Stone." It was a girl's voice, but low and husky. Curious, he turned. It was the blonde —and she was taller than he had realized when he had seen her in the bleachers.

"Oh, I . . . uh . . ." *She must be five ten!* he thought.

She laughed, a deep mysterious chuckle. "See

you." Then she disappeared around the corner of the huge building.

Bucky shook his head in confusion. *What in the world?*

A moment later Dad clapped him on the back. "Well, you got in!" he beamed. "And not a minute too soon!"

His son grinned. "What did you think of that play at the end? Pretty slick, huh?"

Mom gave Rachel Marie a tug. "I thought that boy was shooting it," she exclaimed. "I said to Dad, 'Oh, no, he missed it!' And then I saw you catch it and make the basket."

"You played good, Bucky," Rachel Marie declared, her hand tightly in Mom's.

He reached over and squeezed her shoulder. "Thanks, baby."

"Who was that girl talking to you back there?" Dad asked as they climbed into the car.

The boy shook his head. "I have no idea. She seems to know me, though."

Dad laughed. "You boys have miracle finishes like that very often, and pretty soon everybody in town'll know ya." He started the engine. " 'Specially the girls."

Sitting in the front seat, Mom frowned but didn't say anything.

* * *

"What'd I tell you?" Coach Walker chortled. "Litton and Stone did it for you again! Talk about *déjà vu!*"

The younger coach sat at his desk thinking. "I gotta admit those two guys carry all the rest of 'em. Boy, what a mess," he said, shaking his head. Then he looked up at the older athletic director. "I mean, I figured I'd just let Stone ride the bench. Sooner or later he'd get tired of it and quit." He sighed. "But then when we were down 12 like that, I really didn't have any choice. During practice he and Litton were the only two guys with any court sense to run plays."

"That's a sweet give-and-go move they've put together," Walker observed.

Brayshaw nodded. "Yeah. They got a couple hoops out of that, didn't they?"

The older coach looked directly at him. "Ted, what are you gonna do about all this?"

Coach Brayshaw threw up his hands. "What can I do?" he growled. "After tonight I gotta let Stone play." He snorted. "If I don't make him a starter, folks around here are gonna paste up mean posters about *me* on the walls." He picked up a stopwatch on his desk and fiddled nervously with it. "I dunno, there's something about that kid I just can't figure out."

Mr. Walker sank down into the one free chair in the cramped office. "What do you mean?"

"Well, it's not just that he plays so well." He looked over at the other man. "I mean, there never was any question about that. Baseball and basketball —he's a talented kid. Another Bo Jackson."

"What then?"

Mr. Brayshaw shook his head in bafflement. "Somehow he just sparks the guys up. Even those guys that really don't like him all that much." He cocked his head. "I mean, even riding the bench, he was always boostin' the other players on, taking part in those little huddle rah-rahs we do. Know what I mean?"

Coach Walker nodded. "Face it, Ted, he's a

leader." He paused, thinking. "Every now and then you have a fellow come along who's just plain a champ. Win or lose, he's all champion." Looking the younger coach in the eye, he said, "Your Bucky Stone is that kind of man."

The JV coach nodded reluctantly. "Yeah." He sighed again. "Why him?"

Coach Walker became sober. "You know something, Ted? It's that religion of his."

Brayshaw raised his hands in frustration. "That stuff again," he complained.

"In my mind, there's no two ways about it. With this kid it's 'Chariots of Fire' all over again." His voice softened. "He's out there playing for God, Ted."

After a long, awkward silence, Coach Walker continued, "What're you going to do about the Eagles' game?"

"What do you mean?"

"It's on Friday night."

Mr. Brayshaw's face tightened at the words. "Boy," he muttered, "before last night I was just gonna let Stone have the night off. What the . . . " He looked up. "I figured by then he'd probably quit anyway."

"Well, that's out, now."

"Yeah." The younger coach's face had a dour expression. "Think I should try to get the game moved back to Thursday then?"

Mr. Walker nodded. "Yeah, Ted, I think you should. It's free on our calendar. Why don't you see if the Eagles can switch too?"

"You mean right now?"

"You got something better to do? May as well get it settled before vacation if you can."

Coach Brayshaw pursed his lips. "I guess so," he muttered. Impatiently he pulled the phone closer. Reaching into his desk drawer he pulled out a laminated sheet of school district phone numbers. After dialing, he put his hand over the mouthpiece. "What's their JV coach's name again?"

"Bietz."

"Oh yeah." A moment later the Concord district coach's gravelly voice came on the line.

"Mr. Bietz? Ted Brayshaw here. Over at Hampton Beach."

Sitting against the far wall, Coach Walker listened with interest to the one-sided conversation.

"Well, it's like this," his fellow instructor explained. "We got a kid on our JV squad who can't make our Friday night game with your squad, and I was hoping you could accommodate us with a switch to Thursday. You know, the 14th."

A brief pause. "No, it's not like that." Mr. Brayshaw tightened his grip on the receiver. "It's a religious conflict. One of our forwards can't play on Friday evenings or Saturdays." He cast a glance over at Coach Walker. "No, not Jewish. Yeah, a Seventh-day Adventist." Pause. "I don't know what he's doin' in our school. But he's here, and so I'm tryin' to work this out."

He put his hand over the receiver again. "Grumpy old dude," he growled to his senior coach. "He says most of those 'Advents' go to their own school." Then, in a persuasive tone: "Listen, it's just a road game for you guys. We're the ones who have to shuffle things around to make this work. In fact, we're gonna have to send out a special announcement to parents and the community and everything."

A second later his voice rose noticeably. "Look, we're talking about a ball game, that's all. This fellow's entitled to his beliefs and I'm tryin' to work it out for him." He took a breath. "Can't you give me a break?"

A moment later he replaced the receiver. "They'll get back to us," he murmured.

Coach Walker broke into a laugh. "That was pretty good, Ted," he chuckled. "You sticking up for Stone . . . I shoulda gotten that on tape!"

* * *

The Monday after Thanksgiving, Bucky entered the locker area with a sense of expectancy. Already he was noticing a thawing of the emotional barrier that had separated him from his teammates. He sat down in front of his assigned cubicle and was just about to slip his shirt off when he noticed a note fluttering from the metal locker door. "Please stop by my office. T.B."

T.B. was Coach Brayshaw. Mystified and with a sense of foreboding, he slipped across the hall to the coach's cubicle.

"Coach? You wanted to see me?" Bucky tried to keep his voice steady.

The man motioned him in. For several moments he said nothing, his fingers playing nervously with a whistle cord on his desk. Finally he looked up. "I guess we better clear the air," he said at last.

"OK." Bucky sat motionless.

"First of all, you played a great game last week. That was a terrific five minutes you gave me."

"Thanks."

Coach Brayshaw took a deep breath. "I don't know how to say this," he added reluctantly, "but I guess I should apologize as well for how things turned out last school year . . . and then the beginning of this year." He paused. "I didn't give you a fair shot—and I'm sorry."

"I, uh . . ." Bucky struggled to find his voice. "It's OK," he managed at last. "Really." He forced a grin. "All's well that ends well, Coach."

The sports director nodded. "Anyway, I got a kind of peace offering for you," he said with a small smile. "I just got off the phone with the coach of the Eagles. They've agreed to move their Friday game with us to Thursday so that you can play."

"Do you mean it?" Bucky gasped.

Coach Brayshaw nodded and looked him squarely in the eye. "Glad to have you on board, Stone." They shook hands.

Bucky returned to the locker area tingling all over. To have things resolved with Coach Brayshaw was a miracle he had never anticipated. *Thank You, Lord,* he breathed.

Just then the front door to the complex opened and Dan Litton breezed in. "Stone!" A wide smile split his face as he made his way over to the younger player. Suddenly he staggered and fell forward heavily.

"Dan!" Bucky darted forward. "Are you OK?"

The older boy tried to lift his face off the concrete floor. "Ready to play," he murmured thickly.

Recoiling from the stench of alcohol, Bucky realized that Dan was drunk!

CHAPTER TEN

FIGHT!

Frantically Bucky looked around, anger and disgust rising in his throat. For the moment the locker area was empty. Lifting Dan by the armpits, he pulled him to a sitting position. "Dan! Listen to me!" He licked his lips nervously. "What are you doin' here?"

His friend looked at him stupidly. "Whattya mean? Jusht here for practish." His words were slurred.

"How much have you had to drink?" Bucky's voice had a raw edge to it.

"Dunno. Some beer." Dan's head lolled forward.

For a moment Bucky sat thinking. Finally he stood. "I gotta get you out of here," he announced firmly. "But first I'm going to see Coach Brayshaw."

"No!" For the first time, Dan spoke clearly. Then he slumped forward again. "Coach'll . . . really get . . .

mad." His face flushed as he strained to form the words.

"Tough." Turning on his heel, Bucky crossed the hall to the office he had left so lightheartedly moments before.

"Coach?"

Glancing up from his desk, Mr. Brayshaw brightened. "Yeah? What is it?"

The boy's voice was strained. "Coach?" he said again. "I . . . it's Dan."

The athletic director looked at him curiously. "Speak up! Dan what?"

The boy fumbled for words. "Well . . . that is, he's . . . drunk." He motioned with his head. "Out in the locker area."

"Drunk!" The coach's head jerked back. "Now? In the middle of the afternoon?"

Bucky shook his head regretfully. "He's practically passed out."

Coach Brayshaw's face tightened as he stood up. A second later he sat back down again, glancing at his watch. "Five minutes till practice," he growled to himself. He looked away from Bucky, thinking. Then his jaw jutted forward as he made a decision.

"Look, Stone, you gotta help me," he said pleadingly. "Get him out of here. Now!"

"But I . . ."

"Please! Do you have any idea what this could do to the team? Get him out! I don't care how. Get him fixed up somehow."

The boy's head swam. "I . . . sure." He looked at the coach. "But I don't know how to help . . . someone like that."

The director's eyes were desperate. "Do your

best," he muttered. "You're the only kid on the team who can . . ." He left the thought unfinished.

Bucky nodded miserably. "OK."

Quickly he made his way back to the lockers. To his relief the one aisle was still empty. In a far corner one of the second string players was suiting up but did not appear to have noticed Dan's condition.

"Pssssst!" He sat down next to the drunken athlete. "I'm getting you outta here."

Slowly Dan looked up. "What 'bout practish?"

"Not today. We're goin' home."

"OK." Dan staggered to his feet, his voice thundering in the locker room. "I prob'ly wouldn't play to my peak . . . peak . . . performansh." He smirked at his own clumsiness of speech.

"Shut up!" Bucky hissed. "Just don't say nothin'."

"OK, sh . . . shlugger."

Taking Dan by the arm, Bucky tried to shield him from the view of anyone who might enter the sports complex. Quickly he made up his mind what to do. "Where's your car?"

"Back lot."

Bucky nodded in relief. There was a good chance they could slip to the remote parking area without anyone seeing them. "Give me your keys," he demanded.

For a moment Dan resisted. "I can drive," he protested thickly.

"No way!" Bucky's voice was firm. "I'm taking you home and that's all there is to it."

"OK." At last Dan seemed to accept his situation

Easing him into the passenger seat of the expensive sports car, Bucky nervously slid behind the wheel. With only a learner's permit in his pocket, the trip was going to be clearly illegal. "I don't know what else to do, Lord," he whispered. "Just get us home safely."

Starting the powerful engine, he maneuvered the car slowly out of the high school campus and onto the street. Dan, semi-conscious in the seat next to him, was barely able to point out directions, but eight nervous minutes later Bucky pulled up in front of the Litton residence. Heaving a huge sigh of relief he switched off the engine and breathed a prayer of thanksgiving.

"Let's go inside," he said, climbing out of the car. Opening the passenger door, he helped Dan stagger up the sidewalk and glanced briefly at the ragged lawn. "Are your folks home?"

Slowly Dan shook his head. "Just my dad lives here," he muttered. "Folks divorced two years ago."

Trying the front door, Bucky found it unlocked. They entered the darkened living room. For a moment it was all Bucky could do to keep from gasping. The house was a disaster.

Piles of trash and debris lay everywhere. Several days' worth of dirty dishes sat in the sink or were scattered across the cracked dining room table. The sideboard contained a nearly empty bottle of vodka and several cans of beer littered the floor. A puddle of sticky liquid oozed into the carpet from one that hadn't quite been finished off.

"Dan?" Bucky's voice was softer now, more sympathetic. "How about a shower? Get you sobered up."

" 'K," he whispered, nodding in agreement.

"I'll wait out here for you."

A few minutes later he could hear the shower

running in the next room. Glancing around, he began to pick up some of the debris and beer cans. Fifteen minutes later the living area, while still dark and untidy, bore at least a semblance of order.

A figure appeared in the doorway. Dan managed a weak smile.

"Feelin' better?" Bucky motioned for him to sit down on the now vacated couch.

"Yeah." Dan's voice was shaky. It would take hours yet before his body would be able to get rid of all the alcohol in it. He looked over at Bucky. "Thanks for your help."

Before speaking Bucky looked down at his feet for a moment. "How'd you come to be sloshed like this in the middle of the day?"

A long pause. "I don't know."

"Have you been drunk before? At school, I mean?"

Reluctantly Dan nodded. For a second he hesitated.

Bucky waited. "Want to tell me about it?" Out in the street he could hear an occasional car go by.

For a long time Dan sat in silence, struggling with his thoughts. He seemed to be wrestling with some decision. Finally, as if an emotional dam had burst, he began to talk. "You may as well know it," he began, his words coming in a rush. "I'm pretty much goin' at it all the time."

"Drinking?"

"Yeah." Dan looked away, his face scarlet. "I keep stuff in the car, in my locker . . ." His voice trailed away.

"Drugs, too?"

Dan shook his head emphatically. "Nah. Jus

booze." His voice was tired and still slurred.

"How long has this been going on?"

The older boy gestured around him. "As long as this," he said simply. "My mom left, and my dad started drinking." He paused. "Didn't take very long before it got to be a team effort."

For several minutes neither boy said a word. Almost instinctively Bucky realized that he was in way over his head. Dan needed professional help with his drinking problem. At the same time, he longed to find a way to meet his friend's even more desperate spiritual need. *Help me, Lord,* he pleaded.

At last he broke the heavy silence. "Dan," he began, "I want to help you all I can."

"Thanks." The response was little more than a whisper.

Bucky looked his friend in the eye. A flood of memories—moments of shared athletic triumph —tugged at him. He realized with a start how much he cared about his friend.

"I don't know what I can do to help you beat this drinking thing," he said slowly. " 'Specially with you living here right in the middle of all this." As Dan said nothing, Bucky took a deep breath. "For a long time, I've been kind of waiting . . . to talk to you about God," he said at last. "Waiting for the right time. But I guess that's now."

Dan made an almost imperceptible nod.

"Despite the fact of how you must be feeling right now, I guess you can see now how much you need Him," Bucky added softly. "Nobody can get you through this stuff except Him." He put his hand on his friend's arm. "Believe me, I know."

For a good half hour the two talked about Dan's

spiritual condition. Dan began to pour out his soul to the younger boy. Several times Bucky breathed quick prayers for answers to his probing questions.

Finally he stood. "I guess I better be going," he said reluctantly. He looked out through the dirty picture window at the setting sun. Suddenly an idea struck him. "Why don't you come over for supper?"

Dan's eyes brightened. "Do you think it'd be OK?"

"Sure." Without meaning to, Bucky's eyes scanned the untidy room.

Noticing it, Dan grinned weakly. "Yeah, I know. Pretty sad, ain't it?"

Out in the driveway, waiting for Dan to scribble a note to his dad, Bucky felt for the car keys still in his pocket. He looked up as the other boy came out the front door. "You able to drive yet?"

Dan stood by the car thinking. For a moment the old bravado threatened to break through. "Sure! You kidding?" Then a strange look came into his eyes. Abruptly he shook his head. "I better not. 'Fraid I won't be in condition to do that for hours yet."

Reluctant to take the wheel a second time under less than emergency conditions, Bucky hesitated.

"Why don't we walk?" Dan suggested. "How far is it?"

" 'Bout a mile."

"That'll make up for the laps we missed at practice."

* * *

Two days later Bucky walked toward the athletic complex with new optimism. As he made his way down the sun-drenched sidewalk, his thoughts returned to the evening meal Dan had enjoyed with the Stone family.

"This is great!" the older boy had exclaimed over and over, wolfing down several helpings of Mom's recipes. Bucky grinned now, remembering the bemused smile on his mother's face as she watched him eat. And she had said nothing about Dan's still slightly slurred speech.

It was after supper that Dan had nodded eagerly when Bucky invited him to accept Christ as his Saviour. A lump of emotion came into his throat now as he remembered Dan's stumbling but heartfelt prayer.

He pulled open the door and sat down in front of his locker, twisting the familiar dial.

"Stone?"

He glanced up. Brayshaw stood there with an expectant look.

"Yeah?"

Coach looked around nervously. The room was empty for the moment. "How'd it go?" he asked in a low tone.

Bucky nodded. "Good," he said simply. "I think we got things straightened out."

The athletic director heaved a sigh of relief. "This drinking a pretty steady problem?" His voice was still guarded.

A nod. "Uh huh." Briefly Bucky explained Dan's home situation. The coach frowned in worry. "But things are going to be different," Bucky asserted confidently. He weighed his words, then took a breath and looked at his coach directly. "Dan's a Christian now."

At the last remark, the coach gave a visible start.

As he stared at Bucky, for a moment it seemed the old antagonism might return. "I don't . . . " He glanced around the room again, measuring his response.

Bucky managed a smile. "Don't worry," he said softly. "He can still shoot."

Coach Brayshaw nodded. "Just look out for him," he said, his voice even. "The team needs him bad."

* * *

The next afternoon Bucky boarded the bus for the short ride to the team's first road game. A feeling of optimism filled the air. The miracle win the week before had given everyone a sense of invincibility.

Sitting alone near the back, Dan motioned him over. "How's it going?" Bucky asked as he sat down.

"OK." Dan forced a grin. "Dry for three days."

"Good for you." Bucky nodded encouragingly. "Counseling center found a time slot for you?"

"Yeah."

"Hang in there, man. You know I'm prayin' for you."

"Thanks for the book you loaned me," Dan said, lowering his voice.

The game with the Tornadoes began with a furious exchange of baskets. The home team had the biggest starting five in the league, and a huge wall banner proclaimed their one-word slogan: "INTIMI-DATION!"

During the first timeout, Andy Gorton sank down on the hardwood, breathing heavily. "Man, those guys are fierce!" he panted. "It's all elbows out there." He reached for a paper cup of water. "And that center? Wilson? What a jerk!" He snapped off an oath as he glanced over his shoulder.

"Well, just stick to our plan," Coach Brayshaw

responded, looking up at the scoreboard. "We're only down by two. If they keep this up, some of their boys are gonna foul out."

The second half began with the Panthers still trailing, now by six points. Several times Dan and Bucky tried their patented give-and-go, but twice the other team thwarted the play with a shoulder or elbow. "Where's the whistle?" Bucky muttered to Dan as yet another shove went uncalled.

With just four minutes left to go, the Panthers called time once again. "Just down by two!" Coach Brayshaw motioned. "But Gorton, you gotta watch your step from here on in. One more foul and you're out."

"Man, they're pushin' me on every play," the lanky center complained.

"They're really playing rough," Chris, the little guard, added.

"I know it." The coach's face hardened. "I can see 'em from here." He glanced over at the referees. "Just give me all you got for these last four minutes."

The game resumed with the Tornadoes bringing the ball inbounds. Their tall center elbowed past Andy for an easy layup. Score!

"Gimme some help in there," Andy complained to Bucky as the Panthers made their way up the floor.

"I'll try."

Gorton had a vengeful look in his eyes. "When we set up, you get me the ball," he growled.

Dan dribbled to the top of the key and stopped, scanning the playing area. He lobbed the ball over to Bucky and moved over to set a screen. Remembering Andy's words, Bucky whipped a tight pass into the lane where the center was backing into position.

Taking the lightning pass, Andy threw an elbow out to clear a path to the basket. The referee, shielded from the play, didn't observe the foul. Two points!

The star center of the Tornado squad, rubbing his cheek where the painful blow had landed, came back down the floor, his eyes blazing. Without even waiting for the ball, he headed toward Andy. With a hard shove, he backed into position and motioned angrily for the ball.

"No way, chump!" the Panthers' center grunted heavily, giving the opposing player a healthy push out of the key.

The whistle blared. "Foul!" The stripe-shirted referee pointed at Andy.

"He pushed me first!" Wild-eyed, out of control, Andy swung out at the taller boy. A roar went up from the home crowd.

Instantly a melee erupted as players from both benches bounded onto the floor. "Fight! Fight! Fight!" The eager chant went up from the stands.

Bucky, standing near the sideline, watched in horror as the confused pileup grew in front of him. Dan, somewhere near the center of the pack, landed vicious blows on one of the Tornado players. The two referees, surrounded by the raging players, tried helplessly to pull them apart.

Hesitating for a moment, Bucky turned and walked away from the fight. Dozens of eyes followed him as he made his way to the Panthers' row of chairs along the edge of the court.

Coach Brayshaw stared at him, measuring the quiet, calm strength in the midst of the grappling bodies.

CHAPTER ELEVEN

INVITED TO THE TOURNAMENT!

Holding an ice pack to his left eye, Dan slumped over in the bus seat. "Stupid miserable game," he growled, fatigued rage still in his voice.

Bucky shook his head in frustration. "Boy, they creamed us," he muttered. "Ten points in those last two minutes."

In spite of his injuries, Dan began to laugh. "Man, that center ran right over you a couple of times."

"Hey, I'm not tall enough to play center. After Gorton fouled out, though, we didn't have any choice."

Both boys glanced up to the front of the bus where Coach Brayshaw sat alone, gazing in frustration through the rain-soaked windshield. "Poor Coach probably thought we were gonna go 16 and 0 this season," Dan whispered. Pulling the ice pack away, he turned toward Bucky. "How's it look?"

"What's black and blue and red all over?"

The forward groaned. "Where were you anyway during the fight? I could have used some backup."

Bucky did not reply immediately. "Before the season began, I decided I wouldn't get involved in that garbage," he said at last.

"How come?"

His seatmate glanced in the coach's direction again. Brayshaw was answering a player's question, shaking his head and muttering something Bucky couldn't hear. Finally Bucky said, "Well, I just don't think it ever solves anything, number one. And plus, I want to honor God on the court during every game. I can't do that if I get into fights."

Dan was silent for a few seconds. "Man, there's more to this business of being a Christian than I ever thought."

The next Monday at practice Coach Brayshaw gave the squad a brief pep talk. "You showed good spirit out there last week." His gaze fell on Bucky for a moment. "Except for those last two minutes where we didn't have Gorton, you hung in there close the whole way."

Chris, the squad's sharpshooting little guard, raised his hand. "How come the refs just let those guys hammer away at us like that?"

The coach pondered for a moment before responding. "You're right," he conceded. "I didn't think the reffing was too jet hot myself." He forced a grin, then sobered quickly. "But I'll tell you boys something: those Tornadoes played us real smart." He paused for emphasis. "They knew if they could get

Andy, here, mad at 'em, he'd foul out. Soon as that happened, they had us.''

A stir rippled among the team.

''I don't mind you standing up for yourselves on the court,'' the athletic director went on. ''And pitching in if there's an altercation of any kind.'' Again his eyes fell on Bucky for the tiniest fraction of a second. ''But don't get suckered into a situation where we come out losers as a result.'' He looked directly at his star center. ''Andy, if you'd stayed in that game right to the end, I think we just might have pulled it out.''

His face sober, the lanky athlete nodded.

''OK, that's it. Let's win a few!''

And the Panthers JV squad did indeed go out and begin to win. Four contests in a row went Hampton High's way, as the starting five began to jell as a playing unit. Dan and Bucky keyed rally after rally, running smooth two-man plays and dishing off timely assists to Andy at center and to Chris, whose 20-foot bombs were dropping regularly.

''It's starting to be a familiar refrain,'' began a newspaper commentary by Big Max, Hampton Beach's regular sports reporter. ''Remember last year's hit tune—'Litton and Stone'? This athletic superduo has sparked the Panthers JV team to a 5-1 record so far, good for a first place tie and a ticket to January's Northern California Invitational in Reno!''

''Not bad!'' Dad grinned, putting down the paper. His feet were propped up close to the roaring fire in the fireplace. Bucky, relaxing from his studies and the hectic two-a-week basketball schedule, enjoyed the Christmas holidays and Dad's teasing praise. Though the holidays did seem more lonely with Lisa gone. Her busy schedule at her new school had kept her from writing as often as she had done earlier during the fall.

"How come they never mention the parents of these high school superstars?" Dad interrupted his thoughts of Lisa.

His son pretended to be embarrassed.

"How long is the team up there for the tourney?" Mr. Stone continued.

"Three days. Kind of a round-robin thing, I guess. They aren't part of the regular schedule, so they don't count in the standings."

Bucky's father looked over at him with a twinkle in his eye. "Well, when you get into the NBA, I just hope you'll remember your poor struggling parents and buy your mom and me a nice house like that player for the Warriors just did."

* * *

The bus tires hummed on Interstate 80 as the Panthers headed north for the tournament. Bucky and Dan sat toward the back, discussing a new trick play the latter was hatching up.

"That'll never work," Bucky interjected. "You might fake your own man out, but the center always comes out on a play like that. Every time."

"I don't think so," Dan responded. "Even if he does, Andy can screen him out."

"Well, we'll try it in practice." Bucky resumed the letter he had been writing Lisa.

Two hours later the big diesel bus pulled into a motel parking lot on the outskirts of town. "Here we are, gents," Coach Brayshaw announced. "Real luxury." He laughed. "Four to a room."

"What?" Andy's six-foot-five frame blocked the aisle. "No way!"

"Just kidding." Brayshaw was in a jovial mood. "Two per room, standard arrangement."

Bucky sighed in relief. "Just you and me, my man," he muttered.

"We got about 45 minutes before practice," the coach announced. "Get settled in, then we'll run over for a quick session and some supper. First game's tomorrow."

Dan and Bucky surveyed the smallish motel room with disdain. "Well, I guess we can each have a bed . . . and sleep diagonally," Dan laughed. "Come on, let's have a look at Chris' room."

The next afternoon the Panthers were easy winners in their first round of play. Bucky's assists sparked the team to 47 first-half points, and he even managed to drop a 15-foot jump shot of his own.

"The man can even shoot!" Dan grinned. "Way to can that one!"

Coach Brayshaw had nothing but words of praise for the team after the contest. "Beautiful teamwork!" he emphasized again and again. "You men are clicking together!" He gave Bucky a little nod of appreciation.

The long shower and team supper were pleasant rewards for the grueling afternoon of play. Bucky went back for seconds from the long smorgasbord.

"Well, what's up for tonight?" he asked Dan later.

His friend grimaced. "Well, Coach has us out here five miles from town, so we can't get into any trouble." He shrugged. "Watch TV, I guess."

The pair was engrossed in a program on the motel room's dilapidated set when someone knocked on the door. "Hey, come on in, Gorton," Bucky invited. "What's up?"

The center sank down on Dan's bed. "Oh, I just needed to get out," he said evasively.

Dan raised an eyebrow. "What's the matter? Randolph doesn't take showers?"

"Nah." Andy shook his head. "It's just that, well . . ."

"What?" Bucky prodded.

After a strained silence, Andy said, "Well, don't tell nobody, but the guy's in there snortin' coke."

"What?" Bucky couldn't hide his surprise.

The tall center raised both hands. "Swear to God," he murmured. "Man, I had no idea."

Dan leaned forward. "This his first time?"

"No way." Andy looked at one, then the other. "I guess he uses it all the time. Says he can handle it."

"Oh, man," Bucky breathed. "This is bad!"

"You're tellin' me," Andy retorted. "I'm in there rooming with the guy." He shook his head. "I mean, those magazines are no big deal. I can handle that." For a moment a hint of a smile crossed his face. "But coke? No way, baby."

"Somebody's got to tell the coach," Bucky interjected suddenly.

Andy bolted upright. "No!" He looked over at him. "You promised, man."

"I did not. And anyway, this is serious. That guy could kill himself."

Finally, after several minutes of heated exchange, everyone agreed that Bucky had better tell Brayshaw about it. "Go do what you gotta do," Dan said at last.

A few minutes later Bucky was back, his face grim. "What happened?" Andy wanted to know.

Bucky shook his head. "He didn't want to hear about it, that's for sure," he explained, his voice miserable. "But I laid it on him."

"What'd he say?"

There was a short silence. "Said he'd deal with it when we got home."

Dan nodded. "Guess that makes sense." He looked over at Andy. " 'Fraid you're stuck with it."

The next day the Panthers won a closely contested game after a frantic rally in the last two minutes. Despite his activities of the night before, Chris was in deadly shooting form, especially in the second half. Out of 12 attempts made, 10 found their mark for points, including a 3-pointer to tie the game in the closing moments.

"Terrific, terrific, terrific!" Coach Brayshaw gave the little guard a healthy clap on the shoulder. "Keep up those beautiful bombs!" He looked over at Bucky with a quizzical expression.

Again that evening Andy slipped over to his friends' room after supper. "Same problem?" Dan wanted to know.

"I guess." The center was glum. "He just announced, 'Well, I guess I deserve another party.' So I took off."

Bucky paced the room in frustration. "This is serious! Here we are, tryin' to sweep the tourney, and Chris is gonna blow it."

Dan shrugged. "Well, he was sure hot today," he commented reluctantly.

Andy sat down heavily on the bed. "Well, it's his problem," he sighed. Then he brightened. "How 'bout riding into town? See the lights, maybe invest a few quarters in a slot machine?" He looked at the other two boys. "We could split a cab."

Bucky shook his head. "Forget it. Coach said, 'Stay put.' "

"Oh, he wouldn't care," Andy retorted. "We'd just go for a little while." He fumbled in his pocket. "Blast it. Forgot my room key. Better go get it."

After disappearing down the hallway, he returned a few moments later, a strange expression on his face.

"What's the matter?" Dan asked.

"Chris doesn't answer when I knock."

"What do you mean? Let's go see."

The three of them crowded in front of the door of Andy and Chris' room as Dan pounded on it. No response. "Sure he didn't go anywhere after you left?" Dan asked as he tried the door knob. The lock had not caught shut and the door jerked open as Dan pushed on it, only to be caught by the night guard chain. He looked questioningly at Bucky and Andy. "Randolph? You OK?"

Still no response. Bucky tried knocking now. "Chris, open up! It's just us."

"What's the matter with him?" Andy asked.

Bucky turned around slowly. "I don't know. Something's wrong." A sudden look of fear flashed across Andy's face.

Dan took a quick breath. "I think you're right," he blurted. "Something must be wrong." He pounded on the door. "Randolph! Open up!" He looked around at the others. "Maybe if we all hit the door together, we can break that chain loose."

"What?"

"Just do it!" Dan counted to three, and they slammed their shoulders again the flimsy door. The chain ripped loose from the door.

Looking inside, Bucky gasped.

CHAPTER TWELVE

FUNERAL FOR A FRIEND

Dan knelt beside the still form lying on the floor. "Chris! Chris!" His breath coming in short, anxious gasps, he leaned over and felt along the boy's jawbone for a pulse. His body sagged. "Oh, God!" he groaned, tears springing to his eyes.

"What?" Andy bent over the bed to see. "Is he . . . ?"

Dan began to shake violently. "Call an ambulance," he said weakly, his voice flat.

"But . . ."

"Call an ambulance, man!" Tears welling up in his eyes, Dan climbed to his feet. "And get Coach in here."

Andy bolted out of the room and dashed down the hall.

Bucky edged closer. "Dan . . . " His voice was shaking. "Is he going to be OK?"

Dan shook his head slowly. "I don't think so." He bit hard on his lip. "That coke must have . . ."

Brayshaw's tall figure appeared in the doorway, a frantic expression in his eyes as he clutched Dan by the arm. "I . . . what happened?"

Bucky turned to face the coach. "Is an ambulance coming?"

Ashen, the athletic director nodded. "Is he breathing?"

His face still white with shock, Dan shook his head. "I don't think there's anything . . ."

"What about CPR?"

"I don't know anything about that!" Dan grabbed him by the shoulders. "You do it!"

"I . . ." Awkwardly the coach knelt by the prone figure.

"Just do something!" Dan blurted. "Come on!"

As the coach began to press down rhythmically on Chris' chest, he looked up at the other two athletes, fear written plainly on his face.

For a moment Bucky watched the desperate scene. The victory celebration of the afternoon before seemed worlds away as he watched the futile life-and-death struggle taking place on the threadbare motel carpet.

All at once his knees buckled as he sank to the floor. Tears began to course down his cheeks as he began to shake almost uncontrollably. "Please, God," he whispered, his voice barely audible. "Oh, please . . ."

Coach Brayshaw's words from the night before rang in his ears. *I'll deal with it when we get home.*

"Now it's too late!" a voice screamed in his mind. Looking over at the man's pale face, Bucky could tell that similar thoughts were tormenting him as well.

Outside the thin walls a siren blared. "Thank God!" Mr. Brayshaw gasped. He paused for a second to look down at the lifeless face of the young basketball guard. A grimace creased his features as he resumed the mechanical pumping.

"In here!" Dan motioned to the two attendants. Up and down the hallway doors popped open as curious ballplayers burst out into the corridor. "What's goin' on?"

The flashing red light of the ambulance cast long, pulsating bursts onto the dirty snowbanks by the side of the parking lot. Bucky cast one more look at the still form before turning to the attendant. Lowering his voice, he found the strength to speak. "He's gone, isn't he?"

The white-clad paramedic's face was grim. "I'm afraid so, son."

Looking over at Dan, Bucky gave a little shake of his head. The older boy nodded slowly, his eyes still damp and red with fatigued emotion.

* * *

Bucky leaned back against the headrest of his bed. Over in the corner of the room Dan sat cross-legged with Sam.

"Poor Coach," Bucky managed to say at last, wincing at the memories of the night before.

"Man, that must have been rough, calling Chris' parents," Sam observed.

"Boy, it sure was."

Dan glanced at Bucky. "Were you there when he called them?"

Bucky nodded miserably. "Yeah." He looked over at Dan. "He didn't really ask me to stay with him, but I could kind of tell he wanted someone along."

"He telephone them from the hospital?"

"Yeah."

"What happened with the rest of the tournament?" Sam asked.

Dan uncrossed his legs. His face, still pale from the shock combined with lack of sleep, was slack. "I don't know," he said shortly. "As soon as the police got through with us, we just got out of there. Coach called the sponsors, told them what happened, and said, 'We're leaving.' " He paused. "Most of the team was up all night."

A long, painful silence filled the room. Bucky looked out the window of his second-story bedroom. It was a grim winter day outside. "You know what gets to me?" he said at last.

Neither boy answered.

Bucky looked directly at Dan. "You and I both knew Chris was in there usin' that stuff." His voice had a resigned tone to it. "And we didn't do anything to stop him."

"Man, what could we do?" Dan snapped. "You can't stop people from things like that."

"Yeah, I know." Bucky looked over at him. "But you can at least say something." He took a breath. "At least ask them to stop it. Tell 'em you care. I don't know . . . something!"

"Think that might have helped?"

"Well, it certainly couldn't have hurt." Bucky's voice rose in frustration. He glared at Dan, a bit of fire in his eyes. "Like last summer when you gave me a ride home from work, and then afterwards I figured you had been drinking."

"And?"

"And I didn't say anything! You might have killed yourself . . . and how would I have felt then?" The angry words tumbled out.

The next evening Dan and Bucky sat together in the funeral home chapel for the brief service. The chapel was packed with students. The whole Panther team was there, as was Coach Brayshaw, his eyes still carrying a tormented look. Bucky watched sympathetically as the man spoke briefly with Chris Randolph's mother.

"No dad?" Bucky whispered.

Dan shook his head. "Killed several years ago in a trucking accident, I heard today." His eyes softened. "Guess this leaves her all by herself."

After the service ended Bucky went over to speak to Mrs. Randolph. "This is Bucky Stone, one of our players," Coach Brayshaw introduced him.

The middle-aged woman took his hand. "Thank you for coming," she whispered. Her eyes, even though red with crying, reminded him of Chris's.

"I'm so sorry," he murmured. "It was a pleasure playing ball with your son."

She nodded. "I hope he's . . . happier . . . where he is." Her voice betrayed uncertainty.

The words tore at Bucky's heart. Too late! He wished he could talk with Lisa about how he felt. Surely she would understand.

Out in the parking lot most of the team had gathered around the coach. Silently he looked around at them as they stood there, uncomfortably dressed in their best clothes.

"Thanks for coming, men," he managed at last. "This has been tough, I know, but we'll get through it somehow."

"Coach?" Andy Gorton spoke up. "Can't we get some kind of collection up or something? For Chris' mom?"

"I think that would be real nice. Maybe we can get something organized at school."

"What about the tournament?" another player wanted to know. "What happened with that?"

Brayshaw shook his head. "They cancelled it. Finished."

Bucky took a breath. "Coach, what about the rest of the season?"

The man's face was drawn. "Well, life does go on, Stone," he said, his voice exhausted. "We have a game next Monday and a season to carry on with." He looked around. "Even without Chris."

For a moment, no one spoke. The coach pondered something briefly, then cleared his throat. "I guess a lot of us will be second-guessing ourselves for a while," he admitted. "But if every one of you can learn a lesson about drug use, I . . . " His voice softened. "Maybe something good will have come out of all this." He looked at each player, then added one final thought. "And thanks to each of you for rallying around . . . me . . . during this tough time."

* * *

Monday evening the Panthers took the court with a sense of foreboding. Despite the team's 5-1 league record, Coach Brayshaw and his team knew it would be an uphill battle without the deadly outside scoring of Chris Randolph.

Bucky stood along the sidelines during the minute

of silence the announcer proclaimed in tribute to the fallen basketball player. Deep in his heart, the pain of guilt still lingered.

The team's worries about its diminished scoring punch proved to be very real. The visiting squad jumped to an early lead, then settled down to hold the Panthers on defense. Andy and Dan combined for 26 points, but the substitute guards trying to fill Randolph's spot were ineffective. The final buzzer rang with the home team down by a whopping 18 points.

"Man, we are sunk!" Andy gasped in frustrated exhaustion as they slunk off to the showers. "Guess we can kiss the tournament goodbye."

Dan and Bucky discussed the problem on the way out to the parking lot.

"I'll tell you somethin', Stone," Dan observed as the pair leaned against his car. "You and I are gonna have to pick up the slack."

Bucky shook his head and grimaced. "Man, you know I'm not much of a shooter."

"I know, but we got just three days to change that."

"What do you mean?"

Dan studied him. "Ten games to go, and Panthers gotta win just about all of them to make the tournament," he said slowly. "You're just going to have to learn to shoot more."

"In three days?"

"Three days, baby." He punched Bucky on the arm. "I'm comin' over tomorrow to your place, and you are going to shoot and shoot and shoot." His face creased in a grin. "You got the talent, man. Now you just got to start putting the ball up more."

Dan was true to his word. The next evening—by

porch light—he drilled him for an exhausting two hours. Short layups, 15-foot perimeter shots, driving bursts to the basket.

"Now you're gettin' it!" he shouted as yet another jump shot swished through the net.

Bucky rolled his eyes. "You're just goin' easy on me on defense."

The older boy shook his head. "No, I'm playin' you pretty tight," he pointed out. "I can already see a difference, man."

The next two days the pair managed to slip in several more "quickie" practice sessions. "And don't forget to keep passing!" Dan teased. "You're still the Panthers' leading assist man."

Thursday's rematch against the Cougars was a pivotal game for the squad, Coach Brayshaw pointed out to the nervous team in the visitors' locker room before the contest. "These guys still have that buzzer-beater eatin' at them. They want us bad, fellows." He looked around the room. "I need a hard game from every man here."

"Yeah, do or die for the tournament too," muttered one of the guards.

Coach shook his head impatiently. "Don't even think about that. For us to get into the tournament without Chris would be a near impossibility. Just win one game at a time."

Bucky breathed a prayer as the team walked onto the court. *My best, Lord . . . for You.*

Almost as soon as the whistle blew, it was clear that the Panthers had a new life. Bucky's freshly-developed shooting skills, combined with the team's sharp teamwork and unselfish passing, gave the visiting team a clear advantage. He dished off accurate passes to his teammates, and when the Cougars double-teamed Andy and Dan, Bucky burned the defense by shooting himself.

"Way to go!" Andy congratulated, looking up at the scoreboard to admire the team's 14-point half-time lead. "Where'd you learn to shoot like that?"

In the second half, the Cougars came out determined to swamp Bucky out of the offense, but it made no difference. With the other players left open for easy baskets, the Panthers held a comfortable 20-point lead through the final ten minutes of the game.

"Remember how I told you boys not to think about the tournament?" Coach Brayshaw asked with a twinkle in his eyes. "Well, change that order! Start thinking about it!" His eyes fell on Bucky. "Fantastic game!"

It was three weeks later, with the Panthers still hot at 11-4 and one game left to go, that Coach Walker strode into his associate's office. "You see this?" he growled.

Mr. Brayshaw picked up the memo. "Tuesday, Thursday, Friday!" His head jerked up. "The tournament schedule?"

The man nodded. "Man, here we go again!"

Coach Brayshaw carefully set the small piece of yellow paper down and looked up at his superior. " 'Course that's four games away," he observed, his voice even. "Panthers would have to win Wednesday's game, then sweep those first two before this would even be a problem."

Mr. Walker gave him a tight smile. "Yeah, and it's a problem you're dyin' to have!"

"You're right at that." The younger coach shook his head. "Man, after the funeral, I wouldn't even have thought about the tournament. But I'll tell you, I think we have a real shot at the league championship after all.''

"What are you going to do about this?"

A short pause. "I don't know. Do I bring up the problem now, even though it may never come to pass? Or do I sit tight?"

The graying director thought for a moment. "Well, seems to me the best thing to do would be to bring it up right now. Just in case . . . get somebody thinking about it at least." His face was serious.

"Call the district office?"

A nod.

The JV coach reached for the phone. "Like you said, here we go again." He dialed the number.

"Mr. Stevens?" Without fanfare the coach explained the problem.

"Probably won't come up," he conceded. "But just in case we do get lucky, my player's gonna have a problem with that Friday night game." Brayshaw listened for a few moments. Coach Walker's forehead creased in worry.

"Like I said, it's his religion," Coach Brayshaw explained again. "Stone can't play on Friday night." Again a pause. "Friday afternoon, sure. But sundown is pretty early this time of year." An awkward silence. "No, don't ask me to try to explain that one."

He looked up at Walker and covered the mouthpiece with his hand. "Doesn't sound too good," he muttered.

He listened for a moment longer before answering. "Saturday night, maybe?" Then: "Well, if that's how you want to leave it, OK. But if it comes up later, I just want this whole conversation on the record." He tried to keep his voice light.

"Well?" Coach Walker blurted as the younger coach replaced the receiver.

"The official word is, 'We'll cross that bridge if we ever get there.' " Brayshaw shrugged. "In other words, let's not make a fuss till we have to."

The other coach grinned warily. "Well, let's hope it gets to be a problem!"

Tensions ran high as the Panthers suited up for the final game of the regular schedule. As the win-loss record of the district teams indicated, it was indeed the deciding game. Win . . . and the Panthers were in the tournament!

"Just like a tournament game, then," Dan had observed as he laced his basketball shoes.

Minutes before the team left the locker area, Coach Brayshaw gathered it around him. "Well, fellows, this is what we've been working toward," he smiled, trying to keep the squad loose. "Makin' the tournament." He looked at each player. "I know these Timberwolves are just 5-10, but they're dying to keep you out of the postseason games." He raised his voice just a shade. "Don't let them do that to us!"

"No way!" Andy growled.

"For Chris, then."

"For Chris." The players murmured the words.

As they had before the previous two games, Bucky and Dan slipped off to one corner to pray. "Help us to play in a way that glorifies You tonight," Bucky said. "Whether we win or not, help us to represent Your character in the right way."

The one-sided contest that followed was the perfect tune-up for postseason play. The Panthers ran the opposition silly with fast-break baskets and unstoppable moves around the basket. Dan and Bucky's patented give-and-go routines—run from both sides —had the home crowd hoarsely cheering the team to an ever-growing margin of victory.

"On to the championship!" Dan bellowed as the team celebrated in the locker room after the easy win.

Bucky grinned as he congratulated his fellow teammates. "Good going!"

Coach Brayshaw whistled for attention. "Well, boys," he began, trying in vain to look sober. A wide grin creased his enthusiastic face. "This is kind of fun!"

"Attababy, Coach!" One of the guards raised a fist in the air.

The director motioned for silence. "Tournament next week," he added. "Next Tuesday. If we win . . . next Thursday. If we win again . . . "

"Don't say *If!*" Andy almost fell over in his laughter.

"When's the big game, Coach?" Dan asked the question on everyone's mind.

Brayshaw hesitated. "We're not sure yet. I'm still trying to work that out." His eyes fell on Bucky.

CHAPTER THIRTEEN

EIGHTEEN SECONDS FROM VICTORY

A relaxed yet excited atmosphere filled the campus Monday morning as Bucky walked down the hallway between classes. Even though the junior varsity squad was, in a sense, the school's "second string" team, the student body had rallied behind them for the upcoming tournament. Several students, formerly hostile, now gave Bucky encouraging nods. "Go get 'em, Stone," one hollered, his voice echoing off the concrete block walls of the corridor.

Bucky grinned in spite of himself. "Fickle!" he muttered, shaking his head. People would forgive a winner for almost anything, he decided. He would have to write Lisa about that.

A blast of cold air hit him as he walked past the huge double doors leading to the main administration

building. On his way to the library for his one free
period, Bucky wondered for a moment about Tuesday's contest. And what had the coach meant about
"working out" the championship game schedule?

The library was about half-full. He selected a seat
near the magazine racks and pulled open his geometry book. Suddenly his gaze fell on a strangely
familiar figure.

The Blonde. The girl standing in the bleachers
during that Game One victory against the Cougars.
Several times since that evening, Bucky had instinctively scanned the quadrangle during lunch looking
for her. Now here she was, sitting alone at a table on
the other side of the large study area.

Bucky felt his pulse quicken. Since Lisa had left,
his life had been a frantic round of basketball games
and studying. Still, something inside tugged at him.
Sitting at that library table and glancing over at that far
table, he suddenly felt very alone . . . and very male.

Should I do it? For some reason he thought of the
cartoon character Charlie Brown, always wistfully
thinking about the "little red-haired girl" he was too
afraid to meet.

Scooting back his chair, he picked up his books
and began the long walk across the carpeted room.
His heart beating faster, he approached the girl.

"Hi."

When she looked up, an intriguing glint flickered
in her eyes. "Hello."

Awkwardly he motioned toward the table. "Is it
OK if I sit here?"

A smile. *What a smile!* "Sure."

Several tension-filled seconds passed between
them. "I . . . I've been looking for you," he blurted.

"Since the Cougars game."

"But not hard enough, I guess." Her gaze was unflinching.

Bucky took a deep breath. "I don't even know your name," he confessed.

For a second she didn't say anything.

"Well?"

Abruptly she laughed. "Deirdre." Her husky voice made him tingle.

He cocked his head. "How'd you know who I was?"

She eyed him with amusement. "You haven't exactly had the lowest profile on campus this year."

He blushed. "I guess not." Suddenly he brightened. "Have you been to any more of our games?"

She nodded. "Uh huh. Where you lost to the Tornadoes."

Forcing a grin, he tried to think of a retort. For a moment his mind was a frustrating blank. *Here goes nothing.* After glancing around, he lowered his voice just a shade. "Listen, I've got to ask you something."

She leaned over in melodramatic expectation. "Yes, Mr. Stone?"

He flushed. "This Saturday night. I was wondering . . ."

"There you are!" a familiar male voice interrupted.

Bucky's head jerked up. "Dan!" He frowned slightly. "What are you doin' here?"

His friend instantly sized up the situation. "Hope I'm not interrupting anything?" Then he grinned.

Bucky looked over at Deirdre. That mysterious hint-of-a-smile still was there. He gave her a meaningful glance. *Later!*

"No," he sighed in Dan's direction.

The older boy sat down heavily. "You see this?" He put a slip of paper in front of Bucky.

The sophomore read it aloud. "Round One—Tuesday. Thursday . . . Friday." His eyes opened wider. "Friday!"

"Yeah." Dan's face hardened. "You heard that little routine before?"

A heavy knot formed in Bucky's stomach. "I sure have." He looked over at Deirdre. "I'm sorry," he managed to say finally. "Can I . . . we, pick this up later?"

For the first time she looked puzzled. "Sure. I guess so."

The two boys headed for the building across campus where the coaches' offices were located. " 'Course, we may never get to Friday anyway," Bucky noted, glancing at Dan.

The other boy said nothing for a moment. Then, "Let's see what old Brayshaw knows."

The two walked into his cubicle. "Coach? Got a minute?"

"Sure." Brayshaw looked worried. "What can I do for you fellows?"

Dan put the paper down on his desk. "What about this? The championship game's on Friday."

There was a momentary silence. Bucky looked over at Dan, a question mark in his eyes. Didn't Coach know?

"I know all about it," he responded, answering Bucky's unspoken question. "Just got off the phone, in fact."

"What's happening?" Dan asked.

The coach ran his fingers through his hair. "I

called the district almost a week ago, trying to work this out."

"And?"

"At first they told me, 'Well, don't worry about it yet. Your team may not even get there.' " He looked up. "Which is still true."

"But what if we do?" Bucky finally spoke.

"That's the problem." Coach Brayshaw shook his head in frustration. "The district office called me back. They told me they can't move the game, no matter what teams get in."

"What?"

Mr. Brayshaw scooted back in his chair. "You got eight teams going in, four in our division, four on the other side." He paused. "District doesn't want to go to all four teams on their side, trying to work out a switch on the off-chance that the Panthers might get to that final game."

"Yeah, but what if we do?"

Another shake of the head. "They just don't juggle games for one player . . . no matter what the reason." He shrugged. "And I guess I can understand that. You can't rearrange everyone's schedule just 'cause some player has to visit his grandma that weekend."

"But this is different," Dan protested. "Bucky can't play and that's all there is to it."

Brayshaw nodded his head miserably. "Don't you think I remember that?" he snapped.

Dan lapsed into silence.

"What are we going to do?" Bucky asked at last.

"I don't know," the man confessed. "I just don't know."

Bucky was grim as he donned his jersey for Round One the next evening. Even though it was a "road" game for the Panthers, Hampton Beach High School had a large and highly vocal cheering section sitting in the stands.

"Almost feels like I'm just goin' through the motions all of a sudden," he commented to Dan. "I can't play in the final no matter if we win or not."

"Hey, wait a minute. Things might still work out."

"I don't see how."

Dan gave him a hard look. "Well, it's for sure God can't do anything to fix this if we don't win tonight. Lose this one, and God can take a vacation along with the whole team."

Chastised, Bucky nodded. "You're right. Come on, let's go get 'em!"

The game was a tight thriller from tipoff to final buzzer. Down by five points at the halfway mark, the Panthers staged a dramatic comeback midway through the third quarter. Dan pulled off a dazzling "back door" play, slipping in along the baseline behind his defender to drop a reverse layup. One more big basket and a successful foul shot in the last minute made the difference as the Panther squad came away winners in Round One.

Bucky scanned the stands as the rest of the team headed for the locker room. It was a sullen crowd except for the still cheering Panther boosters at the far baseline. "Don't see her anywhere," he muttered to Dan who apparently didn't hear him.

"Bucky? Got a minute?"

Standing by the runway leading to the showers was Oliver Bendall, feature writer for the Hampton Beach newspaper.

"Sure." Bucky glanced over at Dan. "Catch you inside?"

The older boy shrugged. "Nah. I'll wait for you. Maybe this guy'll take my picture too." He laughed.

"I've seen the playoff schedule," the reporter said. "What are you gonna do if your team wins Thursday, Bucky?"

"I guess you already know," Bucky replied without hesitation. "I can't play Friday night."

The journalist managed a ghost of a smile. "Yeah, I figured that part. How do you feel about all this?"

The boy thought for a second. "Well, I wish I could play," he said at last. "And, of course, I hope we win Thursday, no matter how things turn out in the end." He looked directly at the man. "I guess I'm still hoping—and praying—that things work out somehow."

"What about Coach Brayshaw?" Bendall asked cautiously.

Bucky managed a grateful smile. "I guess I am glad about one thing," he said carefully. "At least this year Coach is backing me on this business."

Mr. Bendall raised an eyebrow. "Is that right?" He made a note. "I'd like to hear a little more about that at least."

For several more minutes he asked questions, making an occasional notation on his reporter's pad. Finally, wishing both boys good luck, he strode toward the exit.

"What do you think of that?" Bucky said.

Dan pretended to scowl. "22 points and he doesn't even ask me how to spell my name."

* * *

Wednesday at lunch Sam plopped down next to his friend. "See this?" He slapped a folded newspaper down in front of Bucky.

Bucky's eyes widened. There, on the front page of the sports section, was a three-column story with the headline: "HIGH SCHOOL STAR CHOOSES GOD OVER TROPHY."

"Oh, boy," he breathed as he read the copy. Mr. Bendall had written a hard-hitting op-ed piece about the district's sports scheduling policy. He remembered the reporter's words from a year ago: *"Someday I'd like to write the kind of story that would help folks in this town realize that our kids ought to be able to participate in school activities regardless of their religion."* A surge of emotion lumped in his throat as he realized that the reporter had now done just that.

"You OK?"

Bucky nodded. He read the last line of the article once again and its challenge to the district's school athletic commissioner. "Two seasons in a row this young athlete has shown tremendous courage both on and off the athletic fields of this district. It is time to recognize and reward that courage. Mr. Stevens, do the right thing!"

That evening Mom read the sports page with a quiet smile on her face. "What a great witness!" she commented.

Bucky pointed to a paragraph in the second column. "That was nice how he pointed out how Coach Brayshaw has tried to help."

Thursday evening before Round Two, the junior varsity coach gathered his team around him for yet another pep talk. "Men," he began, "we've had a tremendous year. Even with the tragedy up in Reno, this is one season we'll never forget."

His face was serious, almost grim. Bucky glanced at Dan, then Andy.

"I want to ask you to do two things for me. Go out and play the game of your lives tonight. Give me everything!"

"What's the point?" one of the backup forwards muttered under his breath. "We'd get skunked Friday anyway."

Coach went on without a pause. "Then," he continued, "I want to ask a big favor of each of you." A tiny grin began to show on his face. "Could you each rearrange your schedules to play in the finals Saturday night instead of tomorrow?"

For a minute Bucky couldn't digest the news. Then his heart leaped to his throat. "What . . . what did you say?"

A broad smile split the coach's face. "Saturday night . . . if we win tonight." He raised a fist into the air. "District just called me half an hour ago."

"How come they changed their mind?"

The man gave a melodramatic shrug. "Oh, I don't know," he smiled. "I suppose 70 or 80 phone calls coming after a certain newspaper article didn't hurt matters any!"

"Now we gotta win!" Bucky breathed to Dan. *Thank You, God!*

For a good share of the evening it appeared that Brayshaw's dramatic news would be a moot question. The Eagles, having split two games with the Panthers during the regular schedule, were pinning Bucky down hard on offense. "No passing, no shooting, no nothing," he muttered to Dan, his frustration close to the boiling point.

"Hang in there. We're just down by six."

Bucky cast a nervous glance at the clock. "Seven more minutes!"

Two spectacular rebounds by Andy brought quick fast-break baskets for the Panthers and a rare jump shot by Bucky closed the margin to two in the closing moments.

"Let's fake our give-and-go play, then feed Bill, here, in the corner," Dan suggested. "They always pack the middle on that play. I think they'll leave him wide open."

"Can you hit it, Bill?" The coach's face was grim.

"I think so." The little guard glanced around. "Somebody get me a good pick."

"Gotcha," Andy growled. "Shoot it soon enough to give me a chance at a rebound shot."

With the precious seconds dwindling away, Dan brought the ball down for one last try. Bucky edged closer to him. He flashed a phony hand signal.

At the top of the key, Dan paused and surveyed the field. Deliberately looking away from the right-hand corner, he faked a pass to Bucky, then flung the ball over to the far sideline.

Bucky gasped as he saw how far out Bill was standing. The referee raised his hand, signaling a three-point attempt.

With unerring accuracy the orange sphere sailed in a high arc toward the hoop. Andy dashed toward the basket for the offensive rebound, but the desperate move proved unnecessary. With barely a ripple of the net, the three-point bomb fell through for the win.

A shudder raced through Bucky as he raised both hands in the air. "Thank You, Lord," he repeated over and over. "Saturday night, here we come!"

In the locker room the team hoisted the diminutive guard onto their shoulders. "Bill! Bill! Bill!" they chanted.

"Put me down," he protested, laughing so hard he almost slipped from their grasp.

"Man, you lucked out," Andy teased him. "You were just supposed to tie up the game with a two-pointer! What a showoff!"

"Hey, it was in there all the way." The guard tried to appear nonchalant.

"Listen to this guy!" someone commented.

A hush fell across the room as Brayshaw stood in the doorway.

"How about it, Coach? Into the championship round!"

The man gave them a brief thumbs-up, but his face was strangely subdued. "Did you hear the news?"

"What?" Dan took a step forward.

The coach licked his lips. "The Tornadoes won their game tonight." He paused. *"Big!"* The group fell silent. "That's who we play Saturday night."

Saturday Bucky and Dan retreated to a far corner of the locker room. "I'm glad we're playin' this one at home," Dan said.

"Yeah." The younger boy looked around. "Last game."

For a moment Dan's face clouded. "What's the matter?" Bucky asked.

His friend shook his head. "Just thinkin' about Chris again," he muttered.

A moment later the pair had their usual prayer. "We don't want to pray to win," Bucky breathed, "but, Lord, please help us to do our best again for You. Help us to control our tempers and emotions," he added as an afterthought.

Unexpectedly, Dan began to pray. "Thank You

for all You've done for me this year. And for all Bucky's help." He paused for a moment, collecting his thoughts. "Be with us tonight."

He opened his eyes, grinning. "Awful hard not to pray to win," he said with a short laugh.

Bucky stood. "Yeah." He reached over and retied his shoe. "I always say to myself, 'What if the other team is praying to win too?' Then what's God going to do?"

The team walked onto a court surrounded by wall-to-wall sound. The diehard Panther fans were prepared to whoop and holler without letup for the entire evening if need be.

The game started with the pushing and shoving expected from the rough Tornado squad. Dan gave Andy a long, meaningful glance: *Don't lose your cool! The team that doesn't get charged with fouls will go on to win!*

Five minutes into the contest the Panthers led by four points without a single foul yet called on the squad. "See there?" Dan breathed hard as they scurried back on defense. "Play cool and we got 'em!"

As the clock clicked toward halftime, however, the Tornadoes made a run for the lead. Their big center, Wilson, drove past Andy for two easy layups in a row.

"Time out!" Coach Brayshaw brought the team over to the sideline for a breather. "We gotta stop their momentum."

Bucky looked around the stands. For the moment the partisan crowd was quiet, waiting nervously. He squinted, looking for Deirdre. Was that her in F section?

"Hold 'em tight till halftime!" Mr. Brayshaw snapped. "Get out there, Stone!"

The second half was an emotional teeter-totter for the crowd, as the Panthers surrendered the lead three times, only to regain it every time. "Can't build up a lead on these guys!" Dan snapped as the team took another timeout with five minutes left in the game.

"Try that give-and-go once more?" Bucky suggested.

"Sure. Right side."

The play, usually run from the left, worked like a charm as Bucky tossed into Dan and then darted toward the basket. A foul on the play added three points to the slim Panther lead.

Then the Tornadoes' main guard, a stubby little player named Rich, went wild. "Unconscious shooting!" his teammates whooped as he put three successive shots through the hoop. Tornadoes down by only one . . . with less than two minutes left.

"Get in that guy's face!" The next time down, Bucky swarmed all over the little guard. The shot went awry and Andy, scooping up the ball, signaled for a timeout, their final one.

In the huddle, the Panthers set up a play for Andy at center. "Get this one, and we're home free!" the coach breathed, exhausted excitement burning in his eyes.

Dan brought the ball down, slowing the pace. Working the 45-second shot clock carefully, he faked a dish-off to Bill, then passed the ball to Andy in the middle.

Disaster! As Andy whirled around to make the short jump shot, the opposing guard raked the ball from his hands. Dashing the length of the court, he laid the ball up and in with one smooth motion. Tornadoes up by one!

During a regular game or a scrimmage, the play would have been just one big shrug. But with a panicked gasp, the truth came pounding home to Bucky. The end of the season was just 18 seconds away.

"Move it!" Acting instinctively, he grabbed the ball and tossed it in-bounds to Andy. The center, startled, passed it right back and headed toward the top of the key.

The roar of the crowd echoed in Bucky's ears. Taking a deep breath, he forced himself to think. *No timeouts left!* He dribbled cautiously. The other team, realizing their sudden advantage, was laying back, playing a tight defense. *No fouls!* He could read it in their faces. *Ten seconds from victory . . .nine . . . eight . . . seven.*

A tingle raced down his spine as he surveyed the field. Dan was covered tight. He looked over at Andy. A defender smothered the tall center, cutting off his access to the ball. Over in the corner Bill was buttoned up tight as well.

The roar of the crowd echoed now, as the frantic fans counted with the clock. "Six! Five! Four!"

It was at that precise moment that the play opened up. Drawing from the distant memory of a late fall afternoon, Bucky saw Dan dart quickly across the key, taking his defender with him.

Now as the dribbled ball came back off the floor and into his hand, he made a quick fake in the charging forward's direction. The guard's eyes followed the move . . . for just that one tiny instant.

Go! Before the other player could react, Bucky

burst past him. Time seemed to almost stand still as he saw his lane to the basket. With new strength and all the force of the tumultuous season poured into one final drive, Bucky drove the ball home. Leaping high in the air, his hand reached toward the rim as he gently laid the ball off the glass and in for the winning goal.

The final buzzer. Bucky couldn't hear the shouts of his teammates because the roar of the crowd was too loud in his ears.

When he struggled to see, he realized suddenly that tears filled his eyes. For a split second, his mind traveled back to the pain of last May's shattering disappointments and his bitter doubts on Graduation Day. His heart overflowed in gratitude as he realized how God had directed events for the greatest good.

Dan threw his arms around him. "I knew you could do it! I knew it!"

Bucky nodded. *Thank You, Lord!*

In the locker room Coach Brayshaw was almost too emotional to speak. "Tremendous job, men," he kept repeating over and over. Finally he motioned for them to draw closer.

"This is a season we'll never forget," he said quietly, looking at Bucky. "I want to thank each one of you for the part you played." He looked around. "Anybody have anything to add?"

Silence hung over the steamy room. Dan shifted nervously on his bench.

"Litton?"

The tall forward looked over at Bucky. "Yeah, I guess I do want to say something." He stood and looked around at his teammates.

"Chris's death blew us all away, and I think we

should officially dedicate this championship to him."
The other players nodded their heads in agreement. In
silence they recalled the tragic, ugly end to the little
guard's life.

Then Dan began to speak again. "And I almost
blew it for us," he added reluctantly, "early in the
season."

Bucky tensed, waiting expectantly.

Dan hung his head for a moment before continu-
ing. "I was drinking a lot," he said, "drinking and
driving and . . ."

The coach had a quizzical expression on his face.

The boy took a breath. "Bucky, here, kind of
bailed me out," he said simply. "I think we all owe
Bucky more than just for a winning basket tonight."

There was a quiet stirring in the room.

"Anyway," Dan concluded, "he helped get me
straightened out. Helped me get right with myself and
with God and . . . everything like that." Again he
looked at each one of them. "You guys know I'm not
a preacher or anything, but . . . I guess you may as
well know I'm a Christian now too." Abruptly he sat
down.

There was a long, almost overpowering, silence in
the cramped room.

"Well, hallelujah," one of the guards remarked
with a crooked grin.

"All right!" Coach Brayshaw snapped as he gave
the player a withering look. "I may not be into
religion like Stone . . . and Litton . . ." His voice
betrayed uncertainty. "But I'm all for anything that
turns men into champions, and that's what these two
players are."

With that he gave the squad heartfelt congratulations and strode from the room.

Bucky turned to his friend. "Not bad," he muttered softly.

Dan said nothing.

It was after their showers that Andy Gorton came up to them. "Good game," he said with a satisfied grin.

"Yeah." Bucky, still on a high from the victory, offered a handshake. "You had a great year, Andy."

Dan, too, congratulated the tall center. "You sure did."

Andy gave him a curious look. "I . . . I guess I never knew you were really into this religious stuff you talked about," he said.

Dan shrugged. "Well, I thought everybody should know."

A hard look flickered in the center's eyes. "Well, that's cool, I guess. But just keep it to yourself, OK?"

Dan raised an eyebrow. "What do you mean?"

The six-foot-five athlete picked up his gear and headed toward the door. "Just don't start prayin' for me." His handsome dark face carried a smile, but his words had a tight edge to them.

As Andy headed down the darkened sidewalk into the cold winter evening, Dan glanced over at Bucky for a moment, then turned and stared at the center's retreating back. "You can't stop me," he whispered.